Making Magic
WITH THE
HIGHLANDER

Kalani Madden

KM BOOKS

Contents

Chapter 1

My fall ended when I crashed onto the pavement, flopping like a ragdoll with flailing limbs. The hard concrete shocked my system with its unnatural rigidity. A blast of exhaust fumes choked in my throat.

I lay there for a long while panting and biting back the urge to weep. I ground my teeth to stop myself from crying out his name:

Callum. Callum Campbell. My love.

A lone siren yee-yawed in the distance, only to die away and be replaced by the ack-ack of jackhammer drills. I was back in the twenty-first century, where people dug up the concrete so that they could lay cables down and vehicles fueled by decomposed fossils could carry the injured and dying to hospitals. The air reeked and the noise was toxic. My beloved coastal Scottish Highlands were lost in space and time once more. I had never noticed before how bad the modern era smelt.

Biting my knuckle to stop my tears, I sat up slowly. I heard a girl laughing in the kind of scornful, hateful way I associated with the bullies from school.

"Oh - my - God. Look at the sad freaking hippie chick! She must have, like, blasted her brain cells on acid last night." Giggles, followed by screams of cruel laughter.

"Oh - my - God, like yes! Like, she should be ashamed of herself. That's the color that I want to, like, do my hair though. Kinda like a Kardashian, like."

The two young girls' voices and stifled laughter faded as they turned the corner. I had landed in the alleyway, and I could see from the signage that it was behind the museum. I was lying sprawled in front of two skip bins full of cardboard boxes and polystyrene cutouts opposite a fire exit. Two emotions fought in my mind to see which one should be remembered first: regret at losing my great love and triumph at having dodged the man who had been trying to ravage me.

My regret was powerful but made softer with the knowledge that I could return to Callum at any time simply by touching my charmstone to the one in the display cabinet in the museum behind me.

A triumphant smile lingered on my lips as I thought of the expression on Duncan Campbell's face as he felt me dissolve away beneath his grubby embrace as the charmstone on his tunic connected with the one around my neck.

It gave me the strength and resolution to stand up. My impact on the pavement seemed to have had no effect on me. There were no bruises or soreness. I had to adjust my ankle-length woolen tunic, lifting and tying the ragged neckline higher so that my breasts were no longer showing; as for my bra, it had been ripped to ribbons by Duncan's greedy hands. There was a distinct winter nip in the air, but nothing so cold as the icy conditions I had just left behind. Still, I decided to remove the wolf pelt cloak, tying it inside the earasaid and then hooking the bundle over my arm.

"I could start getting used to this method of travel," I mused to myself. "At least there are no irritating people sitting next to me on a narrow and uncomfortable seat."

It crossed my mind that I should quickly run back inside the museum to see if I could get back to fifteenth-century Scotland, but suppressed the urge. I had a few things I needed to do before returning to Callum.

Walking out of the alleyway with as much pride and dignity as I could muster, I saw a bank logo I recognized on the High Street. I definitely needed money. A few of the bank clerks looked at me with narrowed eyes as I pushed through the main entrance and approached the help desk.

There was a man standing in front of me, but he kept looking behind his shoulder at me as if he thought my bundle might contain a brick. He finished his business at the help desk rather briskly, then it was my turn.

"Hello," it felt strange to be talking in English again. "I'm in a bit of a pickle. I have an account affiliated with this bank, but I've lost my card and ID. How do I go about withdrawing cash?"

The clerk was very professional as if she saw wild women walking into the bank every day demanding to withdraw money.

"Please can you put your thumbprint in here, ma'am. It will verify your identity."

"Wow, that's a genius idea." I could remember all the sarcastic remarks I had made about fingerprint identification being an invasion of my privacy when I had set up my traveling account and funds, but now I was sold on the technology. After reading the information off her computer screen following me pressing my right thumbprint onto the print reader, the clerk gave a little gasp.

"Och, pardon me! It's you! I mean, you are…you were meant to be…"

I could see the clerk's eyes raking me up and down, her mouth open but with no words coming out. I figured I looked exactly like what those two young girls had been laughing about: some ragged festival goer after a drug-fueled binge.

"Please can you wait here, Miss Campbell? I'll fetch my manager."

But of course, she wasn't off to fetch the manager. She was off to ask the manager to call Scotland Yard."

***

"The only way you're going to get the press off your back is if you give an interview."

The detective who had been handling my case was a normal-looking man who had been dealing with my very abnormal case since I had gone missing for over a week, not counting the few days I'd been in hospital under 'observation'. Secretly grateful to those two young girls who had laughed at me as I landed in the alleyway, I had my cover story down pat: I had left the museum and gone on a binge. End of story.

"Why?" I demanded to know. "It's none of their business! I did nothing wrong! I ate magic mushrooms and fell down a K-hole or whatever."

Detective MacDonnell sighed and rubbed the bridge of his nose by pinching his fingers together. "The Kiwi press are calling us a bunch of Scotch psychopaths, Miss Campbell. Please try and see it from their point of view. You hopped off the train at Waverley, got into a taxi, got dropped off here at the world-famous Edinburgh Museum, and then disappeared into thin air."

"I don't see that it's any of their business," I replied in a sulky voice, crossing my arms and leaning back in my chair.

"It became my business when you - and I quote - 'ate magic mushrooms and fell down a K-hole.' And it became the press's business when it turned out that your granny and parents left you millions of dollars in a trust fund. Do you know who gets that trust fund money if anything happens to you?"

I shifted in my chair, uncomfortable in both mind and body. "I'm nineteen bally years old. So no, I don't know who gets the money."

"Your cousins. Don't you feel sorry for them? They have been pilloried by the press! There have been all sorts of accusations made against Pania and Marama and all your other cousins."

I didn't have a smart reply to that. I loved my blood relations and my late great uncle's de facto wife, Marama; they had been in my life since I was seven years old, and they were all I had. "I'll contact Mr. McKaye and make a will…" my voice got stronger. "And I'll jolly well go and give them that press interview! If only to tell those sharks that they better back off from accusing anyone when…if I go missing again!"

Detective MacDonnell gave me a strange look. "Listen, Miss Campbell, I have a lot of sympathy for victims, but you're not a victim! You're lucky you don't get Section Sixed or forced to pay back all the money the government spent searching for you!"

A lady officer walked to the desk and stood next to me. "Come along, dear. Let's get you tidied up before we get you out there in the press room."

"Look…" I didn't want to leave Detective MacDonnell with a bad impression of me. "I never wanted to come back here again. I mean, I was happy where I was. My cousins are welcome to all my money." Giving a wild laugh and shaking my head, I said, "I can't take it with me, after all."

But all the detective did was give an angry shake of his head and make an irritable pointing gesture with his fingers. The female officer obeyed her superior and hustled me out of the room. She guided me to the ladies' room, handing me a plastic bag full of clothes before closing the door behind her.

The ladies' room smelled pungently of chemicals that failed to mask the bad odors. It reminded me of the midden pit dug into the soft ground far away outside the Loch Awe manor house gates. Every morning, part of my duties had been to empty the kitchen servants' chamber pots and hand the pail to the raker. The poor man would haul the pail to the large wooden barrel on his cart and then go trundling the cart and horse down to the midden. The fancy closed door latrines with their lime powder and sea sponges and sluice holes with gutters that were built into the manor house walls had only been for the ladies and gentlemen to use. I hated the job when I had to do it, but I would have given anything to be back in Loch Awe emptying that slop bucket again…life was not meant to be so sterile and cut off from bodily functions as this new age had made it.

The clothes were cheap off-the-rack items, but I couldn't help but marvel at the close, even stitches that made up the seams before putting them on: legging tights, socks, cheap trainers, and an assortment of tee shirts and sweats. Staring at my reflection in the mirror, I wondered if my new life was easy to see on my face. I was pale, with no color in my cheeks or on my lips. Perhaps I would only bloom rosily again once I was with Callum.

I didn't even bother tearing the tags off my clothes, but I crammed the wolf pelt cloak and castle clothes into the large plastic bag and hoped that no one asked about my preferred attire. After running my fingers through my hair, I stepped outside. "I'm ready."

Detective MacDonnell had already lost interest in the case, so the female officer said, "Ms. Wilkinson, our press liaison officer, will handle the press on our behalf, Miss Campbell. Good luck."

There was no 'thank you' or 'go well'. I got the feeling that I had burned my bridges well and good as far as the Edinburgh police were concerned.

Flashlights went off as I entered the room and sat down next to a lady with a no-nonsense expression on her face at a surprisingly cheap, lightweight table that wobbled when I touched it. "Right, please stick to the agreed arrangement, everyone. Miss Campbell, Staff News would like to ask their question first."

A skinny man with a vaguely Kiwi accent stood up in the front row. "Ella. Don't you feel ashamed of how you left things? Do you have any regrets?" From the critical expressions on everyone's faces, I knew that the officer sitting beside me had gotten her side of the story first, probably while I was changing in the stinky toilets.

I glanced over at the press liaison lady, but she just stared straight ahead, shuffling with the papers under her hands; I wouldn't be getting any help from her, that was for sure.

"Before I answer, please can you tell me how many days it was into my disappearance before your news outlet began blaming my cousins?"

The press room went quiet as they waited for the man to answer. A young woman seated a few chairs away from him used her phone to look at the outlet's news feed. "They waited thirty-nine hours and seven minutes after you were officially declared a missing person, Miss Campbell. The article states that after getting in contact with your lawyer and asking him about who stood to gain the most from your kidnapping or death, it was likely that the next thing the Scottish Constabulary would be likely to do is to speak with Interpol regarding your cousins' whereabouts at the time of the incident...with a special interest paid to your cousin, Pania."

I smiled. "Thanks. Okay," I took a deep breath. "Can someone please give me an idea about what happened at the museum? I'm in the dark." The young woman took the question and ran with it.

"The security guard said you vanished into thin air, Miss Campbell. He came back to fetch you and only found your phone - it had been left open and had an image of the Campbell charmstone on it. The guard proceeded to watch museum video footage with the ticketing staff.

"Apparently, the footage shows you falling behind the display case, but the video feed was blurred by static, so no one was sure. The police were contacted after the museum premises, both public and private areas, had been searched. The porter at Waverley Station, the taxi driver, and the tea lady on the train were all questioned before the search was widened.

"CCTV footage at all exits, doors, and pathways to the museum were looked over extensively - the museum has some valuable exhibits, and the insurance company insists on comprehensive, twenty-four-hour CCTV surveillance. There was a time stamp for when you went into the museum - a few minutes before five in the evening, but there is no footage of you leaving.

"The investigation began as soon as every museum staff member had been interrogated and thoroughly background checked. A missing person report was filed immediately after. And according to the messages and search history left on your phone, there was no indication when the police went through your communications that you had plans to go anywhere or do anything before or after booking into your Edinburgh hotel."

The young woman sat back in her chair; everyone looked curious to hear my answer.

I'd had a good few hours to think about what to say. "I fell; I must have crawled out of the museum, which was the reason why I wasn't noticed. I fell because I was on drugs…hallucinogens; I lost track of time…and lost my belongings along the way."

"Miss Campbell," the reporter began; he was a ratty-faced man with an overbite and a clipped British accent. "The police say that you will not submit to a drug blood test."

"I don't need a blood test - the drugs I took don't stay in the system for very long." I turned my head and saw a dark, slim man standing in the corner with his back leaning against the wall; he had a twisted, sardonic look on his face, and his eyes never left me.

"There were and are no raves or festivals booked in the area, Miss Campbell. How do you explain your disappearance when your image was on all the news feeds?" The ratty-faced man was persistent.

"I must have a very forgettable face. Any more questions?"

The young woman stood up, looking cross. "Miss Campbell - are you honestly expecting us to believe that you, a millionaire teenage girl, traveled to Edinburgh in such a state? The five witnesses - and later suspects - the driver, the porter, the ticket clerk, the museum guard, and the tea lady all say you were impatient to get to the museum exhibitions but acted completely normal besides that."

"I'm very sorry my actions put those poor people on a suspects list. I hope they accept my apologies and understand that I had no control over my actions. As for my cousins, I know they are strong enough to tell those people who like to spread rumors to go to hell and take their suspicions with them! If the police want me to be held accountable for any expenses they accrued on my behalf, I will order my lawyer to reimburse them. My gran told me that I was dropped on my head as a baby."

I stood up. "Now, I think I've answered enough questions for now. Like you said: I'm a millionaire teenager. Aren't we supposed to act like that?"

Chapter 2

Callum Campbell waited for his lady love to emerge from her makeshift privy, but she never came. His eagle-sharp eyesight would not have missed it if anyone had followed her into the thicket of bushes and trees, but Callum understood that Ella would have had to walk quite far into the copse thickets to get the privacy she sought - it would be many more days of winter before the leaves returned to the branches.

"Are we going, sir?" One of Callum's soldiers asked him. It was too bad that the manor house staff had fallen into two opposing camps since Ella's arrival, but Callum would bet all he owned that his men would prove to be the more faithful. He already knew the men loyal to him were better trained; Cousin Duncan's men spent more time in the great hall than they did on the training grounds.

"Aye, in a moment." Callum waited and waited. At one and twenty years of age, he knew enough about the habits of women not to question the length of time his amore chose to take at her privy, but he was a good judge of time and knew this was an unnaturally long wait.

Seeing his men champing at the bit to get going, Callum patted his hand up and down in the air to let them know he understood their impatience before he began walking to the copse. Not more than thirty feet away from the tree line, Callum raised his voice:

"Ella? Ella! Are ye well? Are ye done?"

The trees creaked in the cold wintry wind, and three crows flew up into the gray clouds with harsh cries, frightened away by the way his voice echoed off the trunks and branches. That was all Callum needed to know. He was all alone. If Ella had been busy in the copse, the crows would not have been startled by his presence.

Callum had been a warrior for as long as he could remember. Born in Laird Stewart's lodge down in Bonawe and fostered by Sir Colin from the time he wore swaddling, he had graduated from playing with wooden swords to fighting with steel ones before his eyes had seen ten summers come and go.

Lifting his arm and stepping quietly, Callum loosened the sword hanging behind his back, checking the blade was not stuck in the sheath by the cold. He knew better than to withdraw it right away; carrying a broadsword without need to use it would only put him off balance. He had no idea why his mind had moved to trickery and betrayal so swiftly, but Callum was sure he was not the only man who had fallen under the silver haired maiden's spell.

Callum's heart beat faster whenever he thought of Ella. A powerful surge of passion coursed through his veins like quicksilver at the memory of her sweet kisses. From the first time his scout had emerged from behind the rocks at Bonawe, pushing Ella in front of him, Callum had been enthralled. Indeed, if his uncle had not warned him of the existence of the charm stones and the great power they possessed, Callum would have had no difficulty in believing the girl to be a witch.

Since then, Ella's story had become ever more fantastical to him. A slave girl, a kitchen wench, a lady from a place unimaginably far away; she meant nothing to everyone except to him. She was everything. Callum wished he could smile. He wished he would crest the lip of the dell and find her crouching down there, distracted by a green moss under the snow that had been nibbled by deer. Only he knew she was gone; Callum had been a warrior and hunter for too long to have false hope.

A thin scrap of cloth hung waving from a bush twig like a flag of surrender. As he approached it, Callum saw it was one of those strangely woven garments that Ella had been wearing the first time he met her. Stretching out his hand, Callum lifted it gently off the stick and held it to his cheek before inspecting it more closely. The thin weft and warp and been torn asunder, blowing in the frigid air like strands of a cobweb.

"Duncan." His cousin must have been watching and following Ella since they had left the manor house. The copse would be the ideal place to hide while waiting to launch an attack or watch in which direction they rowed. That he should see the day when a surprise sneaking plan such as this was concocted on Campbell soil - and he had sent her right into the lion's den, or at least he had allowed Ella to wander off into the bushes without checking it first or escorting her to the spot. And now she was gone.

He looked up as two of his men crashed through the bushes behind him, their swords drawn. 'Hoots, lads," Callum growled, "how many times have I told ye to hold back from drawing yer swords until ye kent what's on the other side?"

The men-at-arms ignored their captain's jibe but sheathed their swords all the same. "Duncan?" his second-in-command asked, eyebrow cocked at the scrap of cloth in Callum's hand.

"Aye, the very same. Fetch the horses, Andrew. Stay with me, Eamon."

The men obeyed. "Keep yer eyes on the ground," Callum advised. "I want to ken how many o' the busterts were here and where they took her."

Eamon scratched his beard, a considering expression on his face. "Ye think they carried her off...er...would nae that high-arsed rascal do her right here?" Eamon checked his captain to see how well his words were being received and decided to risk continuing to speak. "He could have done her right here and been on his merry way before ye were none the wiser. In and out, so to speak. Taking her off with him does nae make any sense - Duncan is nae the sort o' man to make a show of his sculdudrie."

Callum said nothing by way of reply. He kept his head down, staring at the light scattering of snow on the ground. Then he spoke. "They were on horseback an' wearing their finery." Beckoning Eamon over, Callum pointed to the tracks. "See here is Duncan's poulaine tread. No other knight keeps his points so long."

"Aye, but it will take more than that to convince the elders," Eamon cleared his throat, spitting onto the ground. "Snow melts, after all, and that's no' even counting the possibility that they deem the act appropriate on one such as that girl. She's had no offer of a man's protection...yet."

Again, Callum did not reply. "I have a fair idea what horses they were riding, which means I ken who are the likely riders - although I would nae put it past the artless tallow catches to use another man's horse. Come, the ground has yielded to us everything it will."

Stuffing the cloth into the fur pouch attached to his belt, Callum climbed out of the dell.

Having said his mite, Eamon kept his silence. He did not want to risk a buffeting from his captain. Ordinarily, Callum was the most level-headed of knights, but a man would have to be blind not to see the warrior was hard-bitten by love.

Andrew was coming toward them with three horses. Callum swung himself into the saddle and spurred his horse into a gallop. After darting a hopeless look at Andrew and shrugging his shoulders, Eamon followed his captain at a slower, less mad-cap pace. "Is there hope he will find her intact?" Andrew shouted at him, cantering hard behind. Shouting back over his shoulder, Eamon replied. "How long d'ye kent the captain for ye to understand he will nae care aboot such trifles! All he wants to find out is whether the maiden is safe!"

"If she's still a maiden, I'll eat me woolen bonnet!" Andrew shouted back.

The men-at-arms followed their captain past the gatehouse and into the stables. They found Callum already there, walking up and down the stalls with two ostlers, feeling which horses were warm and sweating.

"There were half a dozen of 'em," Callum announced as his men dismounted. "One of ye return to the barracks, gather all the men loyal to me, and arrest all three of the McCaws, as well as Erskine and Gilroi. Stick 'em in the cellars and draw the bolt on the outside - leave them with no torch."

For as much time as those soldiers working for Duncan had spent at the palace, they had spent an equal amount of time being trained by Captain Callum Campbell. It was no small order he had commanded his two men-at-arms to carry out. Eamon and Andrew looked at one another before Andrew spoke. "I will go. Ye, Eamon, ye go an' stand by oor captain."

The two men briefly clasped each other by the forearm before Eamon trotted off to join Callum. They walked into the great hall together, but the dais chairs were empty. "Where is my uncle?" Callum demanded the steward to tell him. The man looked up from the scrolls of parchments, and the clerks seated around the board with him. "It is no' yet dinner, Captain Callum. I believe there are still two or three more candles to burn before the bell rings."

Cursing under his breath, Callum flung out of the great hall. "I'll hunt the rat doon in his chambers."

Duncan's chambers were on the second floor of the manor house, next to his mother's retiring room. "Och, the whelp should learn when to cut the apron strings," Eamon grumbled under his breath, "but then who would Milady Campbell advise to dress so fine in the mornings?"

Callum said nothing: his mind was too focused on the task ahead. Not bothering to knock, he lifted the latch on Duncan's door. It had been bolted on the other side. Stepping aside, Callum let Eamon announce them.

"Duncan," Eamon said in a casual way. "Can ye lift the latch for me, please, sir? That silver-haired she-dog has gone missing an' yer faither begs us to search the castle. He seems to have taken quite a shine to her."

Callum stepped out of sight; he knew all of his cousin's tricks and spyholes. Duncan had been away from the manor house for so long, Callum had as much time as he needed to comb through the Campbell heir's chambers at a leisurely pace. He had found all the spyholes and secret panels a long time ago, so he waited in the shadows, sure that there was no angle through which Duncan might see him.

But their ploy worked; the sound of a latch being drawn back could be heard, and then Eamon's voice speaking out, clear as a bell. "Losh! Sir, who were ye expectin'? Why d'ye have four armed men sitting here with ye?!"

Callum watched his second-in-command amble inside Duncan's chamber, his tone pleasant and teasing. "I did nae ken we were under attack, sir! But I cannae report back to Sir Col until I've set me eyes around yer rooms."

Duncan's voice came back. "Did me cousin go carryin' tales to me faither? I swear, I did naught."

Continuing his jovial chatter, Eamon could be heard to say, "Naught about what? There is only the suspicion that the ungrateful she-dog took advantage of the captain's trust an' ran away. We believe Callum's head has been overruled by desire, but not enough for no' to be mighty peeved at the wench's disappearance."

Duncan grunted. "Och aye, I'll give the girl that; she's as comely as they come, but she's a witch. 'Tis a great pity, for she would have adorned me mattress well."

"A witch, ye say?" Eamon's teasing tone did not leave his voice, even as Callum could hear his second-in-command opening large chests and peeking behind tapestries. "Why d'ye say that?"

One of the other men in the room spat out the words. "Because, ye great ox, the girl lately disappeared in front of our very eyes! I've heard tell o' such things, but to see it in the flesh - God's teeth. The sight froze the marrow in me bones!" There was the sound of someone drinking heavily and a mug being slammed down on a table.

Callum had heard enough. Withdrawing a dirk from his belt and the sword from its sheath, he strode into his cousin's chambers. Duncan gave one irate squeal when his four armed guards promptly dropped their weapons and backed up against the nearest wall with one man even trying to climb out of the window casement.

Pointing the tip of his sword against Duncan's throat, Callum waited for his cousin to speak first.

"Ye would nae dare!" Duncan breathed. "I'm the heir."

"I doubt if ye will be able to continue callin' yerself that in heaven, cuz." So said Callum, entirely at his ease. Eamon gave up his sham searching and went to watch the shivering men by the window. Callum nodded to let his soldier know he must not drop his guard. He had taught the Campbell soldiers all the tricks to get out of a tight corner. "Or will ye care to lay me odds that ye don' end up in the other place?"

Duncan slowly patted his hands down in the air in a placatory gesture, but Callum did not lower his sword. Sighing, Duncan decided to give up. "Och well, ye have me. But it's no' me who'll hang for what was done. As God is me witness, cuz, the wench disappeared. I requested a dalliance of her and she refused and then vanished. We all screamed so loudly, I was sure ye would hear and come running right awa'."

Withdrawing the torn breast binding from his pouch, Callum asked through gritted teeth, "And how would yer 'request' go about explaining this?"

All the men in the room bent closer to stare at the ripped lycra sports bra. "Of what substance is that?" one of the guards queried. Callum ignored him and continued waiting for Duncan's answer.

"I kent ye were spiriting her away afore I had a taste o' her market wares, Cal!" Duncan was half cross, half ashamed. He was beginning to feel that he had done something wrong. "Mither told me that ye were closeted with Sir Colin for a goodly while. We kent ye were plotting something, some way to harry the wench away before the priest arrived."

It was plain to both Callum and Eamon that Duncan must have been on the lookout for Ella for a long time. The moment she emerged from the kitchens, it was her undoing.

"So aye, I did touch her, but no' much. Ye ken how finely pounded oatmeal floats on top o' water before melting away like snow in springtime? That's how she left. One moment I had her clutched to me bosom, and the next - naught."

Callum wanted to drop to his knees, the agony he felt inside was so real. But he withdrew the tip of his sword blade from his cousin's throat a fraction. "Is there anything else ye want to tell me, cuz? Afore I tell yer tale to me uncle."

"Aye," Duncan loosened the tight chemise ribbon around his neck with one finger before continuing. "Aye, she was wearing an amulet exactly like mine on a cord around her neck."

Chapter 3

"Okay, but how much can I carry inside the pack with the flotation device in the pocket? Will I sink without it" Ella was back at the camping, hiking, and outdoors store, but this time she wanted to buy a waterproof backpack.

The shop assistant was trying to be as helpful as they could, despite some of Ella's more curious requests. "Have you seen that episode of Bear Grylls in the wild where he takes off his jeans and ties a knot in the legs and then pulls air into them to create a flotation device? You could always do that instead of traveling with the floatation device in your pack. That is...unless you *deliberately* want to fall into water...?"

Ella shook her head while smiling. "No thanks, I've had enough of cold water to last me a lifetime. But I need the flotation device in there. It's to help me rise to the surface more quickly." The assistant scratched her nose. "Yeah, but if your pack is too heavy, you will still struggle to come up for air."

Ella hadn't told the assistant that she had put in an order to buy Krugerrands and a few British Britannia one-ounce gold coins, and was not sure how much they weighed. She also had her earasaid and wolf pelt cloak to stuff in. "Umm, okay, what's the maximum weight I can carry before the flotation device fails?"

The assistant went off to find out. Ella saw the girl and her manager looking over at her as they spoke; she knew they recognized her. For the rest of her twenty-first century life, Ella had accepted that she would forever be known as the teenage millionaire who went on a drug bender for over a week without telling anyone.

For the last three months, Ella had been busy with such shopping sprees. After being recognized by the staff at the outdoors equipment store, she took to wearing light disguises. Sometimes they worked, sometimes people would catch a glimpse of her silver hair under the baseball cap and point her out to their friends.

The dreary Edinburgh winter had turned into a damp spring as she honed her medieval survival skills. Waking at six every morning, Ella would sip hot cocoa as she took a lesson with Professor Helmsby. He was Head of the History Department at one of the most prestigious universities in England and knew enough about linguistics in the Middle Ages, from reading medieval church records to being able to teach Ella everything she needed to learn.

That morning, Ella stirred her hot cocoa with a loving look on her face, followed by an expression of exquisite delight as she took a sip. "Always with the cocoa, Ella. Fond of chocolate, are we?" Professor Helmsby asked Ella over the computer screen.

"Professor, you have no idea how much I'm going to miss it," Ella said before gripping her quill in preparation for the lesson.

The Professor was used to Ella's quirky statements by now. "You passed the medieval alphabet test I set for you, Ella. Now, there might be a few regional discrepancies on the southwest coast of the Highlands in 1452, but you will be able to read any Bible or church records - the script the clergy used was fairly standardized by then.

"Now, on to pronunciation. Your vocabulary is quite a mishmash. From the west coast words you have already told me you know, I gather the main language spoken in your area of interest arrived there from Ireland somewhere around the fourth century. But there is enough Old English in there to categorize it as Scottish."

"Aye," Ella began to speak fifteenth-century 'Inglis-Scottis' in a deliberately slow way. Life had a more measured pace back then; Ella had to learn to draw out what she was saying, especially when talking in public. She had heard great uncle Colin and her gran speak Gaelic to one another growing up at Glenorchy, so not all the mellifluous words were unknown to her; she just had to learn to recognize them in context.

The Professor had told her at the beginning of their lessons: "The western isles of Scotland, specifically the Gaelic Kingdom of Dál Riata in Argyll, had long been connected to Ireland. Two sides of the same coin. But the language had all but disappeared by the middle of the fifteenth century."

The private lesson continued until mid-morning. The professor's alarm went off, and he stopped. "I think you are well on your way to understanding the fundamental grammatical syntax and vocabulary of the region and era, Ella. 1452 is a very exciting time in history: the end of the Middle Ages is widely recognized to be the year 1500. Your year of interest is on the cusp of our Modern Period. I can't tell you how refreshing it has been to have such a keen student."

"Thank you, Professor," Ella said brightly. "I will remember you every time I speak to my clan."

"Goodness!" Professor Helmsby babbled excitedly. "Your whole family talks Medieval Scottish?! We must form a society! Perhaps we could revive a Scottish play or do a blog?"

Ella barely suppressed her giggles. "Thank you, Professor, but no. My family doesn't have the internet. But on an entirely unrelated matter…you wouldn't happen to have come across any mention of the Knights of Cronos during your studies by any chance?"

After asking Ella if she knew the spelling - which she didn't - the Professor gave her an approximation of the spelling, 'Khronos,' and then asked her if she had tried online. "Not with the new spelling, no. I've been trying it spelt with a 'C'."

They both tapped on their keyboards and confessed to coming up with nothing. "It sounds like ancient Greek, which is not my area of expertise, Ella." Professor Helmsby proffered his advice. "Try the local library or ask on Quora. But you must understand that after such a long time, we can only take a blind stab at what its spelling or association might be."

After bidding the Professor a very fond farewell and switching off her cheap, new laptop, Ella skipped outside to find something to eat. She had tried to stay in a hotel beyond the Edinburgh city limits, but she found herself becoming very agitated if she went too far away from the museum and so had settled for staying at the Waldorf Astoria Caledonian Hotel instead. At least there, she could be sure of the door-men keeping out the press.

It was less than a mile's walk to the museum, and Ella was not surprised to find her footsteps were taking her around Edinburgh Castle hill, past the cemetery they had used to film a famous scene in the Harry Potter franchise, and thence onward to the museum: she was drawn to the other half of the charmstone like a magnet. It was lucky the museum restaurants served good food!

"It almost feels like I'm going out on a date," Ella murmured under her breath as she placed sunglasses over her eyes and tucked her hair under a baseball cap so that no staff would recognize her. "Because the closer I sit to the charmstone, the closer I am to Callum." And she walked into the lobby to eat at the Museum Kitchen restaurant once more. During her first week back, Ella had bought an anonymous credit card and loaded it with enough money to buy a National Museums of Scotland membership under a fake name.

No longer would Ella bury her head in a book while seated at a table. She wanted to look around and try to find something about the twenty-first century that she might miss in the future - or the past: Ella was no longer sure which was which.

After ordering a toasted sandwich and soda - she was definitely sure she would miss ice-cold sodas on a hot summer day - Ella sat back in her chair, looking around the room. She never got tired of the neat array of orange banquettes and pale yellow stone walls, both classic examples of modern interior decoration in heavy-traffic areas.

A movement caught her attention. A man had been staring at her and then quickly looked away, anxious not to catch her eye. Without thinking, Ella touched the charmstone under her sweater - it was her most treasured possession - but she relaxed when she recognized the man's face. He was the dark, slim man from the press interview, the one with the twisted, sardonic face. His expression was the same when he realized she knew who he was. Inclining his head toward her and nodding, the man lifted up his soda and raised it in her direction with a questioning look on his face.

Her cover blown, Ella decided to take the high road and indicated to the man that it was okay for him to sit at her booth. Bringing his drink with him, the man sat down opposite her. They observed one another in silence.

"I see you are an old hand at this game," the man said.

Ella frowned as she stared down at the ice in her soda. "I suppose you want me to say 'what game?' whereupon you can insert your opinions into my thought process."

The man laughed. "Ah. Yes. I see. A very old hand. I was referring to your disguise."

"It wasn't much of a disguise if it didn't keep you away."

At that, the man gave up, trying to look unconcerned. He sat forward, leaning his elbows on the table, nearly knocking his glass of soda onto the floor. "How much do you know?" he asked Ella earnestly.

That caught Ella's interest. Did this man suspect her drug story? There were still so many rumors and conspiracy theories about her disappearance online: aliens, Illuminati, ghosts, Scottish Independence fanatics. It reminded Ella of a cross between Indiana Jones and the Da-Vinci Code. She had been sure to watch the security footage from the museum; it had been uploaded onto multiple platforms. The blizzard of static that blitzed the screen at the same moment she disappeared did seem extraordinarily convenient. It was only a matter of time before someone began to talk about time travel.

"Look, I'm not a teenage smartass - my gran would be disappointed in me if she thought I had become one - so I'm going to stop acting like one. I only do that because…well, because it's kinda expected of me. But how much do *you* know?"

It seemed like a reasonable enough question to ask him under the circumstances, but the man's lips closed into a straight line. Ella was fed up now and didn't care who the man told about her disguise. "Show me some ID before I - before I leave."

Rolling up the sleeve of his shirt, the man showed her a mark on his right wrist. It was pale red and welted. Ella had leaned in to look at it before she realized what it was and recoiled in disgust. The mark had been branded onto his skin. It looked like a foreign word: Κρόνος.

"What does that mean?" Ella didn't know why she was whispering, but it seemed like a good idea to do so.

"Do you not know? Did your gran never tell you about us?" The man had also lowered his voice.

Ella was fed up and even a little bit scared. If this man was about to expose her, it might be even more difficult for her to return to the museum - and return to her love. "This is beginning to sound like Twenty Questions," she tapped her finger briskly on the table. "Tell me who you are, or buzz off."

"I am one of the guardians of the charmstone. The shattered stone on display inside this museum. My name is Satellius."

Pleased to hear that one-half of her charmstone had its own society of fans, Ella relaxed. "Oh, why didn't you say that you were a charmstone fan from the start? It's a lovely little historical artifact, isn't it, Mr. Satellius?"

The man's sardonic smile returned. "Yes. Have you managed to discover the crystal's secret history yet?"

Ella answered his question with another question. "What is that word you have burnt into your skin?" The longer she looked at the raised brand on the man's wrist, the more excited Ella became because the letters resembled ancient Greek.

He ignored her question. Sighing and looking around the dining room in a nonchalant fashion, Mr. Satellius said, "Ella Campbell, did you know the museum is removing the charmstone from the display cabinet tonight?"

She couldn't help but give a little scream. Clapping her hand over her mouth to stop more signs of her distress from escaping, Ella managed to get out one sentence. "How do you know?" All the other questions she wanted to ask the man evaporated, driven away by panic.

Mr. Satellius sighed again. "I have sworn an oath to know such things. What do you plan to do? You must have known this would happen. As good as it is for business having the crystal on display for everyone to come and see where the drug-addicted teenage millionaire fell, the Board has decided to remove the exhibit."

Ella was sure this was a trap. If she believed him, he would tell the museum staff, and then they would be waiting for her later when she returned, as she knew she must. But what if this man was some kind of an ally, beholden to help her because of the fan club he belonged to?

She had no time to lose. She needed to get back to the hotel for her backpack. "Thank you. It was nice to meet you, Mr. Satellius." Ella stood up, moving to the cashier to swipe her card, but the man was there before her, striding from the booth to the cash till in a flash, where he grabbed her upper arm.

"I would go well for you if you take my advice, Ella Campbell. Take both this time."

Ella shook his hand off her arm. "I'm not interested in taking anyone's advice, Mr. Satellius."

Ella said goodbye to the man politely and walked away. He had been so intense Ella could not resist looking back over her shoulder to check the man was striding after her, but to her relief, he had gone.

As she was about to duck past the ticket donation office again, Ella paused. "What are the odds that the man who issued me my ticket then will be on duty again today…? I hope he isn't."

Ella's luck was in: a plump-faced, red-haired lady was sitting at the booth. Ella joined the lunchtime queue, hopping from foot to foot as the people in front of her asked touristy questions. Finally, she reached the booth.

"Hi...I'm looking for the charmstone display? But I don't have time today - can I come tomorrow?"

The lady shot her a look of extreme impatience and displeasure. "It'll be gone tomorrow. And please don't bother telling me that you're an influencer with fifty squillion followers online, because I can't help you. This is a museum, not a pilgrimage."

Thinking to catch more flies with honey, Ella changed tactics. "Oh no, I'm not one of *those*. I'm studying geology and was interested in what type of crystal it was inside the silver casing."

The woman smiled. "Honestly, I'm sorry for being short, but those pests are downright creepy. We caught one of them with his pockets full of Geiger counters, infrared thermometers, and EMF sensors! All those - we call them charmstone pilgrims - were causing a disturbance for our younger visitors, so the amulet is being put into storage until all this blows over."

"Er...any idea how long it is likely to be in storage?" Ella wanted to know, thinking it might be better for her to wait out the fuss over her disappearance.

"Oh, the Board says about four or five...years should do it."

Ella opened her mouth to ask another question, but the door inside the booth opened, and the ticket booth man from her first museum visit shuffled into the small kiosk, balancing a cup of tea in his hand.

"Oy! You're-"

He got no further before he was talking to thin air. Ella was pelting down the pavement as if vicious hounds were running her down.

Chapter 4

To Ella, it felt as if she didn't draw breath until she had reached the hotel. Frankly, she was getting tired of always having to look over her shoulder. She relaxed the moment the doorman opened the entrance doors for her and she stepped into the cool, air conditioned lobby.

After adding air conditioning to the things she was going to miss about the modern era, Ella walked into her suite and headed straight for the closet. On the luggage rack and hangers were several more disguises.

"Okay…it's probably time for me to start looking like one of those charmstone pilgrims."

Tapping her front teeth with one finger, Ella hummed as she craned her neck to look at the packets of Halloween outfits she had bought. Deciding that a blue bob wig would be the best way to blend in, Ella moved to the mirror to try it on. "I'm definitely going to leave this wig in the loch water before I rise to the surface," Ella reminded herself. "It can pass as an interesting piece of seaweed. I wonder what the lifespan of these blue fibers is?" She didn't want to be the first person in history to dump plastic waste into the ocean.

A few more packets were ripped open, and the contents were put on before Ella deemed herself good and ready and moved to the mirror. The blue wig was very artificial and anime-looking and not at all like the blue hair dye she saw on some students and young people walking aimlessly around the streets, but it would have to do. She had glued and hooked two dozen fake piercings over her face and ears, finishing off the image she wanted to present with a temporary tattoo on her neck.

Fishing a wand of liquid eyeliner out of her makeup bag, Ella applied the black over her eyelids and temples in long, sweeping strokes.

The look was perfect; she was unrecognizable as the pale blonde nine-teen-year-old from what seemed like so long ago.

Clothes next. Her scullion servant clothes were already stowed neatly in the backpack along with her other medieval items. All she had to do was fetch the gold coins from the hotel safe. Ella had been in a state of readiness for a long time, almost like a pregnant woman when she reaches the final months before the baby is born and feels safer sleeping with her overnight bag next to the bed.

She had commissioned a medieval recreationist to make a suit of clothes for her, but Ella was not too worried about authenticity: so long as Sir Colin and Callum believed her backstory, Ella was sure that no one would dare question the origins of her clothing too closely.

A chemise of undyed, roughly woven linen was waiting for her on the hanger. Ella liked to smell the fragrance of the natural fibers as the garment fell over her head. She had been surprised to learn that linen was about as far from cotton as could be. In fact, the fabric had more in common with the hemp ski pants she had been wearing on her first fall back in time, than it did with cotton. Linen was made out of flax fibers, flax being a wonder plant that was stronger and more ab-sorbent than cotton, with antibacterial properties to boot.

In addition to the chemise and other functional fifteenth cen-tury clothes, Ella had commissioned a high waisted, soft blue dress, or gamurra, made from finely spun wool and lined with a green linen kirtle underneath it. The neckline was a plunging V-shape, more to show off the green kirtle under the dress than to expose her bust, and the long sleeves were detachable. A houppelande, veil, hood, leather laced-ankle boots, and patterns were all crammed into the backpack too, alongside the fur and earasaid.

Remembering the main aim was to get close enough to the charmstone to connect the two crystals, Ella tucked the chemise she was wearing into a pair of black lycra-cotton blend leggings and pulled a mid-thigh length, baggy black, long-sleeved tee-shirt on to hide the chemise. Setting the nylon wig straight with a couple of tugs and heft-ing the backpack over her shoulders, Ella was ready.

There would be no sunglasses or baseball cap this time. Those items were too obvious when it came to disguises. This time, Ella would be the embodiment of a young girl who had her own ideas about why that wacky teenage millionaire had disappeared.

Stepping out of the elevator, Ella approached the clerk on duty at the reception.

"Hi. Just checking that you have my passport and stuff in the hotel safe." The clerk gave her a friendly look. "Ma'm, if that's where you stored them, then they will still be there. We have a very strict protocol."

"Good to hear," Ella said, with only the faintest tremor in her voice. "Listen...I've had these flashbacks, you know, from when I did all those drugs. I guess some of them must have been acid..."

The hotel staff knew all about Ella's adventure: not because they followed the news, but because she had told them after booking in. "Don't worry, Ms. Campbell. If you need help, please contact reception at any time of the day or night."

"Thank you," Ella felt bad about lying to the kind hotel staff, but she had to go. "But in the event of me possibly having another breakdown or flashback and-and maybe disappearing again - we can't rule that out, not after last time - I want to leave my phone here. And-and if I don't come back, just go ahead and post those letters I left in the safe with all my papers."

The smile had melted off the receptionist's face. "Ms. Campbell! If you're feeling like that, we must get you to a hospital at once!"

But Ella was already backing away from the desk counter. "No, I've never felt better. Please don't worry about me - ever. All the stuff you'll need is in the safe: my lawyer, my cousins, and the trust fund details. Just in case. Thank you."

Pushing out of doors, Ella began retracing her steps back to the museum. Never had she been more aware of civilization and industry before. "Goodbye buildings. Cheerio pavements and street lighting. Farewell, my dearest, *dearest* public toilets and faucets."

Knowing the strategy she wanted to use, Ella loitered outside the museum until she saw the people she wanted. Falling into step with a family of one-weekend dad and his three bored and listless teenage children, Ella started talking to the eldest teen, a girl slightly younger than she was but with purple-dyed hair.

"Hi, are you also coming to see the charmstone?" she asked just as they were walking up the steps to the entrance. The girl's eyes lit up. "Oh - my - God. I forgot about that! Hey dad! Can we go see the charmstone exhibition?" Turning around to see that his daughter had gained a companion, the father looked harassed and talking in a strong Scottish accent, he replied. "Och, that auld story? Aye, sure, if we have time."

"But I want to go see the seal intestine jacket, da'," the youngest teenage son whined in a complaining voice.

"Och, aye, aye, whatever," was the exasperated father's reply. "Just don't tell yer mither I forgot yer asthma pump."

And so, all the man issuing tickets saw this time was a frustrated father and four teenagers coming to spend an afternoon at the museum. He didn't bat an eyelash when the two teenage girls with blue and purple colored hair walked past. Later, after Ella's escape, he was able to answer with all honesty that her disguise had fooled him hook, line, and sinker.

So near and yet so far, Ella heard a raised voice telling her to stop. Putting an innocent expression on her face, Ella turned around. "Who? Me?"

Waving her goodbye, the teenage family disappeared into the inner museum halls. "Aye, you. You can't go in there with that pack." A security guard had his hand up to halt Ella's progress. Her heart began beating faster as her mouth went dry. She should have known that security would have been amped up after the last time she came into contact with the charmstone.

Putting on her strongest Kiwi accent, Ella said politely. "Please, I can't leave it. I'm backpacking around Europe, and it has all my papers and cards in it."

"Then go back to the station and hire a locker, but you can't enter with such a large bag. We have some extremely valuable artifacts on display."

You don't have to tell me that. But the only thing Ella said out loud was, "Okay, just give me a-"

There was only one thing to do. Ella sprang into a sprint, the heavy backpack pounding her back and chafing her shoulders. She was sure that even with the added weight, she would be able to dodge the security guard if he came after her. Dashing past another guard, Ella heard his walkie-talkie crackle. The man looked torn on whether to answer the person contacting him or chase after Ella. He chose to answer the walkie-talkie. As she charged across the smooth, white marble floors, Ella heard the guard shouting. "Yes! She's gone past me now." Before the sound of pursuit began in earnest behind her.

Only a few more steps. The display cabinet was in front of her.

Too late, she saw yet another guard belting across the hall to cut in front of her. Everything seemed to slow down around her as Ella realized her escape back to Callum was not going to happen. The charm-stone display would probably never be on show again, that's even if they didn't prosecute her or lock her away for a long time.

Panting and sobbing, Ella tried to duck around the guard, but it was useless. He was reaching for her backpack to pull her to the ground.

Only, he never reached her. With pounding steps and one great leap: Mr. Satellius tackled the guard to the ground, shouting at her, his eyes bulging with panic.

"Do it, Ella! Do it at once! Connect the stones! Take *both* stones with you!"

Ella blindly did as he told her. Lifting the amulet from her neck and lunging at the display glass, Ella pressed it against the transparent barrier. Immediately, the stones reacted to each other. Everything turned dark, the air crackled with electricity, and the room and people around her began to fade away.

But this time, Ella gripped both stones before she began to fall into nothingness.

***

It was the strangest sensation. As the two stones became one, they seemed to relish being next to each other again, throbbing and glowing happily as their auras embraced.

Trusting in the backpack's flotation device, this time Ella waited patiently for her head to break through the surface of the water, pleased that she didn't have to remove her pants and trap air inside them like Bear Grylls.

She was still shocked at her behavior back at the museum. It was one thing to imagine flouting the rules and quite another thing to do it. The guards' faces and attitudes had reminded her of every single person with an inclination toward overbearing authoritarianism and who somehow always managed to find employment in areas that bestowed unlimited power on them. Instead of putting her down as a worried backpacker who was too paranoid to leave her bag in a locker, they had gone ahead and treated her like the Unabomber.

A rushing feeling let her know that she was underwater, but Ella could feel that it wanted to eject her at the top. As her head broke the water surface and air filled her lungs, Ella found herself still panting frantically, the adrenaline stubbornly refusing to leave her bloodstream.

There was a good reason for this. As Ella clambered out of the water and onto the shore, she saw she was not alone. A man was waiting in the shadows of the rocks. He was dressed in common medieval clothing: calf-length surcote split in half at the hem and draped over light chainmail with a leather hose tied above his boots on his belt, but there was a well-spruced look about him that made Ella pause. And somehow, he reminded her of the man who had helped her with the charmstone back at the museum. His hair was not as dark, but his skin was bronzed, and his expression equally meditative with a slightly supercilious quality to it. His body language was keenly observant, but relaxed, non-aggressive. When he did not move or say anything, Ella allowed her alarm to lessen.

Wading closer to where he was leaning against the rocks, Ella hailed her watcher, pleased to be able to speak her first Scottish words.

"Are you an ally of Mr. Satellius'?"

A grim smile broke across the man's face. "How goes my old friend, Satellius?" The man twisted his wrist around to expose the strange letters branded across the veins close to the palm of his right hand. The wound looked recent; it was so raised and red, protruding from the skin like an angry welt. He spoke modern English, and this shocked Ella. After all she had been through and struggled to learn, she wondered if she had simply been transported to another space, not another time. Inhaling the air, she could smell no pollution.

"Please tell me this is the year of Our Lord, 1452?" Ella hoped it sounded as if she knew what she was doing and there was no panic in her voice.

Nodding his head, the man beckoned Ella closer. "Yes. I gather Satellius did not get the opportunity to tell you all?" Ella shook her head while shrugging out of the backpack and laying it on the pebble beach. "We hardly spoke, and when we did, Mr. Satellius was very cryptic. I gather you gentlemen know how the charmstones work? Do you have a couple of stones of your own that you're using?"

"I wish it were that simple," the man said. "I have been here only once before - to monitor the consequences of an astonishing action. I can assure you that you are experiencing the effects of something that was started a long time ago…something that should have never happened."

It was clearly spring, and from the blackened ruins of the old brigand camp in the distance, Ella guessed three months or so had passed since Callum's men had attacked it. Thin, verdant tendrils of spring vines looped and crept over the desolate camp remains, and small buds were bursting from the branches. The air, when she inhaled, had that fresh, clean smell she remembered so well: the scent of untarnished oxygen wisping and curling over the hills and dells.

She was satisfied the stones had done their job. "Do you have any idea where I might find passage upriver?" Ella asked the man politely, wishing it was easier to open the backpack straps without breaking her fingernails. "The water has risen quite a bit since I was here; the snows have melted. It would really help me a lot if you could show me where the closest village is."

She stood up, waiting for the man to answer her, but he was gone.

Chapter 5

If someone had disappeared as if by magic behind Ella's back six months ago, it might have given her pause for thought, but as things were now, all she did was shrug.

"You have mysterious friends, Mr. Satellius," Ella said to herself, staring hard at the rocks where the man had been standing with the shallow waves lapping close to his feet. Thinking she couldn't trust her senses, Ella plodded over to the damp sand and looked down. There were two boot prints. As Ella watched, the incoming tide washed the prints away until the beach was unblemished once more.

Looking up at the sky and tracking the bright disc of the sun behind the clouds, Ella gauged it was nearly three o'clock in the after-noon. She had gone on an extensive survival training course back in the twenty-first century and had no fear if she had to spend the night outdoors.

Hefting the pack onto her back and walking to the scene of the battle, Ella's gaze drifted from side to side, looking for more recent signs of activity. She found plenty of them.

A spear stuck into the ground, not far from where the scout had dragged her over the rocks to stand in front of Callum.

"So, you have been back here, my love, and left me a sign." Wrapped around the spear shaft was a thin woolen ribbon of plaid. It matched the plaid of the earasaid Callum's sister, Margaret, had given her. The weapon made a satisfying shushing-shicking sound as Ella pulled the shaft out of the sand. It had been buried deep, so deep the waves would have never been able to wash the spear away, no matter how high the spring tides came in.

Making use of what light was left in the day, Ella pried open the paracord tied flaps of her backpack again and retrieved her Middle

Age clothes. For some reason, and even though she knew her raiment was probably above her station, Ella wanted Callum to see her dressed in her pretty clothes. The wide cuff openings of her houppelande were dragged and so long they almost dragged on the ground.

She had brought a tiny mirror with her and used it to rid her face of the last traces of makeup, tattoos, and fake piercings. Looking back on things in hindsight, Ella supposed that she must have looked *exactly* like the sort of person who went around throwing paint on priceless objects d'arts, and regretted her scornful preconceived notions about the Edinburgh Museum security staff; the giant backpack she had with her now was nothing at all like the small canvas holdall she had crammed one change of clothes, ID, and cards into during her first museum visit.

Running her fingers over her face, Ella checked that she hadn't missed a piercing. It was bad enough that she was going toward people who had witnessed her melt away in front of their eyes without adding dark makeup and facial markings into the mix. The blue bob wig was gone, probably floating downstream. Hopefully, it would not stop until it reached the Atlantic Ocean. There would not be much left of her modern persona once she took off her clothes.

Stripped down to her chemise, Ella covered it with a plain brown kirtle and Margaret's wool tunic, adjusting the garments, so the neckline of the kirtle showed above the tunic.

She had worn in her plain leather laced ankle boots already and supplemented their comfort by adding a pair of soft woolen curthose to her feet. After rigorously hiding her hair under a plain linen hood and wrapping the plaid earasaid around her shoulders, Ella believed herself ready.

Not only had she put the past three months to good use, but the Scottish Highland spring weather was everything she had expected it to be. The sound of birds twittering amidst the tree boughs was almost deafening as she walked closer to the ruined campsite. An ominous cairn of stones covered that part of the shoreline, and Ella knew very well what she would find under the sand if she dug deep enough. Observing the ground around the cairn with a calm, almost detached manner, Ella noticed the sand had been scraped away in between the cracks of the less heavy stones: signs that scavengers had been busy excavating the bodies.

Thinking it to be as good a place as any, and after checking she had everything she needed for her hike to the castle at the top of the loch, Ella dug away the sand after displacing some of the stones. She needed to hide her backpack, which was now the least authentic part of her guise. The stench of death and decomposition became more intense the deeper she scraped at the sand, but Ella gritted her teeth and continued. She was no longer that bewildered teenager from the mega-sensitive modern age.

Her task finished, Ella stepped back to check if anyone would be able to see any sign of her hiding place. She doubted whether folks would be willing to venture to this coastline, not with the sorrowful-looking cairn as a mournful marker. This close to the water, any medieval Scotsman worth his salt would be thinking the beach would be the ideal place for the maighdean-mhara Selkies and the Blue Men of Minch to gather on a quiet Spring evening.

A dirk, a flint, some pure copper and silver coins, and small amounts of spices wrapped in twists of waxed parchment were in the silk pouch hanging from her belt. Her charmstone was safely around her neck where it was in no danger of hurling her back to Edinburgh.

Ella had studied this area on Google maps so many times it felt as if she knew every curve and bend of the river on a personal level. But coastlines and estuaries, in particular, change over the years, so she would not take any chances trying to cross from Bonawe to Loch Awe's river mouth. She must tramp along the beach until she reached the boundaries of Laird Stewart's land. Ella was sure she could blag her way into Stewart Lodge by dropping Callum's name. The Laird was meant to be his father, after all, wasn't he? Ella wished she had paid more attention to what Callum had been saying to her as they rowed upriver that first time together.

Orienting herself the way the ex-SAS survival skills teacher had shown her how to do, Ella began the ankle-twisting tramp to Bonawe. Scottish springtime temperatures were no walk in the park, and she needed to find Stewart Lodge before sundown.

Not long into her hike, Ella noticed a longboat drifting past. Squinting her eyes to block out the westering sun, she saw a hunched shape sitting in the bow.

"Hie!" With her freshly forged dirk in the pouch hanging from her waist, Ella was far more confident than a helpless young lassie without one. "Whither go ye?"

The man immediately changed his course to be closer to the shore, where he might converse with Ella without shouting. "Whither d'ye seek?"

"Kilchurn Castle - Loch Awe."

The man sucked his lower lip for a wee while, thinking about the distance. "It's oot o' me way, but I will take ye upriver if ye pay me and make me the offer o' hospitality for the night."

"I cannae guarantee ye shelter, sir," Ella thought it best to be honest. "What if I offer to buy all yer fish instead?"

They struck a deal, and the man rowed closer to the shore. As dreadful as it was to wade into the chilly waters, Ella did it willingly. She was so close to seeing Callum again she could almost taste his mouth pressing down on her own. Being taken all the way to the waters lapping the castle causeway was far superior to seeking out Callum's father.

Ella knew all about the fostering system in place among the upper classes in Medieval Scotland. Sometimes, young lads of noble birth were sent to neighboring knights to foster good relations between the nobility; sometimes, they were raised on farms from the time they were infants, the farmer's wife providing dual duties of wet nurse and mother. But the aim of most fostering was two-fold: it enabled the noble lady to get back into the business of birthing bairns as soon as she could, and it caused the child to grow up without airs and graces. The time to meet Callum's father would have to wait.

The fisherman gave her a hand up into the boat and did not drop his hand after she got in, keeping it held out for one of her precious silver coins. Ella knew that much silver weight was far more than the fisherman could hope to earn after six months' worth of fishing, but like everyone in the modern era, she felt compassion for anyone with their palm held out in supplication.

He bit the coin before placing it in his pouch and, satisfied that her request was legitimate, set to pulling on the oars after pointing the prow toward Kilchurn.

The sun was westering quickly now, still yellow but brushing the tops of the tall trees that lined the riverbanks. How well Ella recalled this trip made before in all its winter glory. Now tree boughs were bent with heavy blossoms and new green shoots poked from previously barren twigs.

Even taking into account that it would be another three hundred years before the Julian calendar was superseded by the Gregorian one, and thirteen days were lost forthwith, Ella could tell the atmosphere was far colder now than it had been back in her modern era.

But that was their problem now, not hers. Ella craned her neck, waiting for her first glimpse of Kilchurn Castle Tower as the oars dipped and pulled in the black loch waters.

***

It was full eventide by the time the boat knocked against the causeway post. Ella recognized one of the urchins wading in the river mud, searching for crabs to sell as bait.

"Greetings, lad," she beckoned him to come closer. "How would ye like to have all this man's fish? But in return, ye must give him shelter for the night."

The wee lad's mouth dropped open into a perfect oh of astonishment. "Surely ye are jestin' me, lady? A day's catch o' fish is worth a fortune."

She shook her head, ruffling the lad's briny-smelling hair. "Nay, I would nae jest about such a thing. Go, take the man to yer cottage and request yer mither to stoke the fire - yon fish must be smoked to keep it whole."

Leaving the fisherman and young boy to strike their own bargain about who would gut the fish, Ella began the long trudge over the hillside and down to the manor house beyond, but she froze in place when she noticed the thin cascade of newly erected stairs jutting out from the castle tower's narrow doorway inside a recently built wall of stone. It was an impressive defensive watchtower now, five stories tall, with a half-finished courtyard wall encircling the rocky outcrop where the tower house stood. Its outline reminded Ella of late-Victorian industrial chimney stacks, similar to how the artist, L. S. Lowry, painted his urban landscapes.

Checking the chimney, she saw smoke. Calling back over her shoulder, Ella shouted. "Hie! Has the household moved back to Kilchurn?"

The boy shook his head and then came trotting closer so he could whisper. "The household is divided, lady. Sir Knight lives here and her Ladyship lives at the manor house yonder…"

Smiling, Ella thanked the boy. She wanted to tell him how amusing she found the medieval version of the man being forced to sleep on the couch, but refrained. She was dying to know the full story behind the split, but wanted to see Callum a million times more.

Dodging around the wall stones, Ella dithered which entrance to use. The boy was watching her and shouted, "Hasten, lady! The tide comes."

Ella had never been to the castle during high tide before. She was shocked to see how quickly the water was inching toward her feet. The causeway was slowly sinking under the waters, and the fisherman's boat seemed to take on a life of its own as the waves lifted and moved it closer to the shore's edge.

Throwing caution to the wind, Ella ran up the narrow stairs, trying not to dwell on what would happen to her, and she fell over the balustrade-less sides onto the jutting outcrop of rocks below. When she got to the top landing and looked down, the black loch waters were already lapping the first step of the stairs.

Her knock was answered by a calm-looking servant, his status in the household displayed by the pewter-carved wolf emblem pinned on his doublet. "Greetings, sirrah," Ella put on her best 'visiting a Knight's castle' voice. "Please announce me to Sir Colin: I am Ella Campbell, back from the Norse lands."

This time, there was no sentry on duty to slam a pikestaff in front of her nose. Any invasion would have been so obvious because the countryside was clear to see from miles around. The men-at-arms would sound the alarm the moment an enemy stuck their nose over the mountain ridge, which would give the soldiers at the manor house barracks plenty of time to trot over the hill.

Once inside the first level of the watchtower keep, all the servant did was point to a stool where Ella could sit down. Then he shuffled off to deliver her message to Sir Colin's chambers. It was late enough in the evening for the household to damp down the kitchen fires and retire, but Ella remembered some of the gentlemen and ladies at the manor house had liked to sup in the manor house's great hall if the fire was still burning.

Too amped up to sit down, Ella wandered around the entrance chamber, searching for the masons' marks that had been engraved into some of the stones. Pushing aside the tapestry that hung over the great hall entrance, Ella peeked inside.

It was a magnificent hall beyond what she had imagined the middle ages level of comfort to be. It was the first instance of Ella thinking: now, *this* is what I call Renaissance art.

Two massively tall candlestick holders stood like sentries beside the entrance, their hulking presence obviously there to intimidate any dubious visitors. As for the candles inserted into the tops of the warm bronze pillars, they could have burned for a year without wicking out; they were thicker than her thigh and longer than her legs. Even in the modern era, the candlesticks' worth was incalculable.

The hall's interior was more of the same. Richly carved, highly polished tables and chairs were pushed back against the walls because no items of furniture could be left in the middle of any room in case someone walked through the chambers and bumped into them in the dark. The chair seat cushions were plump, stuffed with goat and horsehair, and embroidered with pure gold lamella threads looped over the silk to form sparkling hoops. A small round side table caught Ella's eye. The base was some kind of red mahogany wood, crafted to resemble a mythical Grecian animal: half lion, half eagle, but with the breasts and face of a fierce woman. A luxurious wool rug was spread over the flagstones instead of threshed straw, woven with rare colors, maroon, plum, and blue.

But what dominated the room the most was a massive portrait hanging on the wall - the first thing anyone would see as they came in. The painting must have been done by an Italian maestro. The chiaroscuro technique was flawless, enough to make the life-size portrait seem lifelike and three-dimensional. The subject was a serenely beautiful woman with her eyes demurely staring at a point on the ground, her hair hidden behind a tight cap covered with thin lawn linen. Anyone would be forgiven for thinking it was the Virgin Mary until closer inspection showed Ella the signs of matrimony. One of the subject's slim white hands was holding a section of her kirtle demurely at girdle height to bring attention to her belly, and there was a statue of the Greek goddess Hera, on the mantle in the background. Her jewelry was ornate and looked very expensive, with a colored stone on every finger and a gold cord necklace as well as the gold embroidered girdle. These were hardly symbols that would be found in religious art. The Latin etched onto the marble of the mantlepiece announced the woman's title: Marriott: Lady of Loch Awe and Glenorchy.

Ella had never visited the Kilchurn castle during her three months back in the modern era: it would have been way too macabre; she had read about the 'ancient' structure online.

The servant returned, beckoning her. "Follow me."

He did not lead her to the great hall but to one of the tower's spiral staircases instead, climbing from flight to flight until when Ella got a glimpse out of the window, all she could see was the rosy sky-line. The servant scratched on the wooden door panel, then bowed and began climbing carefully down the steep stone steps again because of the length of his poulaines. He took the torch with him, leaving Ella in the gloomy darkness.

Hearing the latch lift, Ella tilted up her chin and prepared to sweep into a low curtsy. It had been three months; she wanted Sir Colin to know she was no longer suited to work in the kitchens.

An imposingly tall, dark shape blocked out the light of the wood-fire burning inside the room. As her eyes grew used to what little evening light was filtering through the tower windows, Ella's vision saw a rough, russet beard, wild red locks, and the same blue eyes that had been haunting her dreams for weeks.

"Callum." Ella threw herself into the Highland warrior's arms.

Chapter 6

After spending so much time apart, of course Ella had plotted and planned out exactly what she wanted to do when she saw Callum next. But all of that flew out the window when she was faced with the reality of him. Sweeping her into his arms, Callum carried Ella further inside his retiring room, placing her down gently onto one of the ornately carved armchairs next to the fire. He was shocked but completely taken by surprise. She supposed that the utter conviction that they were destined to be together was as strong in Callum as it was in her.

"Yer hands are cold, lass," he rubbed her arms and fingers in between his own strong, warm ones. "Let me call that useless servant back here to fetch ye a bowl o' broth."

Ella shook her head and, after stumbling over the words in disbelief at her boldness, managed to say, "No, please. Take me to your chamber, Callum. I never want to see Duncan again until I am your de facto wife." Then she blushed and hung her head. She did not have doubts that he would reject her, but Ella was scared he might think her a saucy jade for being so forward.

But part of love was showing the other person that they are desired and needed more than anything else in the world, and that meant they must join their bodies together. Still, Callum hesitated, torn between his intense desire and the indoctrinations of the medieval church, and after complimenting her on her command of Scots English, he said. "But lass - me own dearest Ella - I have so many questions. I dared to hope ye would return, just as me uncle promised me ye would."

She loved the way his Scots burr made the Old English words sound richer and more melodic, but Ella was not to be distracted. "I've made up my mind, Callum. Make me your wife in deed before we bother about making it so in words. I shall not leave this room until I am sure there is at least one thing that dratted cousin of yours can no longer take from me."

Callum growled out the words as he fell on his knees in front of her chair. "I prayed that damned Duncan was telling me the truth - that ye disappeared afore he could ravish ye - and yet now ye want to place me in the same light?" Callum buried his head into her lap, clutching at her kirtle with an anguished grip.

Running her fingers through his hair like Ella had wanted to do for so long, she was emboldened to lure him into bedding her. "Callum, my offer will not waver, but nor will it wait. If you think I have traveled across time and space to have my maidenhead ripped away from me by your pestilent cousin, you are much mistaken in the matter!"

It was all the affirmation he needed. Standing up, Callum stretched out his hand toward her. After taking a deep breath, Ella placed her hand in his and followed him to the chamber. This was to be their wedding night. It was far too dangerous for her to be skipping around the Glenorchy countryside without Callum's banner of protection over her. As his vassal, no one would dare to touch her without his permission. This one act would stake his claim on her forever.

With the only light provided by the fire and the only noise the crackling of burning logs, the young couple prepared for their beddan - that ancient ritual that bonds a man and woman together with blooded sheets.

Darting a quick look over at Callum because she was suddenly too shy to stare at him, Ella could see from the natural way he lifted off his chemise to expose the perfectly sculpted chest of an active youth that Callum was unaware of his exceptional male beauty. His torso skin was pale, but his forearms showed the first touches of a light suntan. Immediately, Ella was reminded of the most masterful Italian sculptures, and when Callum casually cast off his breeches and hose, this image of him was confirmed - in all but one area. Once he was naked, Ella dared look at him no more.

The bed was not set up on a dais; the wooden floorboards were sturdy enough to support the bed frame, but a short ladder of steps was pushed against the bed to help those short of stature to climb on top. With shaking hands, Ella removed all her clothes but left the thin linen chemise shift dress to cover her slim body and the charmstone around her neck. Her knees were shaking. This was not how things were done in the modern era. There was no alcohol, no chit chat, and no skirting around the issue of using protection in case the other person was secretly hosting a long list of nefarious diseases or when they had last been tested.

Callum patted the mattress beside him. He had his head propped up on one hand as he leaned his elbow against the long feather bolster as he watched her undress. "Come lass, I won' bite. Would ye like me to run doon to the kitchen to fetch an egg?"

This caught Ella's attention so much that her curiosity forced her to climb up the steps and crawl closer to him. Nestling her back against the arch his body created, knowing that it would be easier to talk to him while she was facing away from his penetrating gaze, Ella lay on her side, trying not to squeal as his hand began to slowly move under her chemise. "Why do we need an egg?"

She felt him shrug even as his hand moved gently over her thighs and hips. "It mimics the juices inside a woman - makes it easier for her to stand the pain."

He must have felt her shiver and paused the movement of his hand as it ventured toward the gap between her legs. "Och lass, we dinnae need to do this, ye ken. I love ye too much to hurt ye."

That made Ella turn around, creeping her arms around his neck. "Callum, I was this - I want you - *so* much."

He kissed her, and that was all the touch Ella needed to know that she belonged to Callum in every single way. He was confident enough in his abilities to please her, but not to a point where Ella felt he was going through the motions. She had a very strong suspicion that this was Callum's first time in bed - or anywhere else, for that matter - with someone. There would have been no teenage parties for him to have honed his skills, but their lovemaking could not have been less like the blind leading the blind. Their communion with one another was more like the biggest, most important exploration and experiment of their lives.

And it was glorious, or at least it was the second time around when they had become used to the rhythm of each other's bodies somewhat, and Ella's anticipation of the pain had lessened.

After the midnight bell sounded in the castle bell tower, Callum wrapped his plaid around his waist, stepped into a soft pair of rabbit fur buskins, and padded down to the kitchens to fetch them some pottage.

Ella fell back with her head on the feather bolster, exquisitely happy with her new medieval life.

"Let the chips fall where they may," she whispered into the dark.

***

They decided it was too late to talk about their plans for the future, but Callum said he could not sleep until Ella told him about her vanishing.

"It sounds like the wastrel was tellin' me true," Callum mumbled after she finished telling him her story; he was chewing the end of a hazel twig to soften the pith before using it to brush his teeth. "But I shall no' forgive Duncan for all that."

Ella knew from her studies that raping and pillaging was something that invaders did and not an action courtly knights and villagers inflicted on each other. In fact, it was more likely that a maid would lay a complaint against a man for flirting with her and not seeing the wooing all the way through to the end! With the church having the country in such a strong grip, forcing a woman to do something against her will was a rare event, especially in such a confined neighborhood as Glenorchy in the Highlands. She asked him if there were any unforgivable sexual sins, but he assured her the church would forgive anything once it was confessed and atoned for.

"Sure, we are aware that there are some men who lust after a comely wench even with a faithful wife waiting for him at home," Callum's voice was slowed down as they lay in each other's arms, watching the embers glowing in the dark. "But nae man is goin' to prowl around a wench's bothy after she has shown herself averse to his blandishments. His pride will nae stand for it."

"So…no rape or adultery?" Ella whispered. Her eyelids felt leaden. It had been a tumultuous day and night.

"Me Uncle Colin lived with Lady Margaret in the state o' fornication for many years, Ella. But he married her after Duncan was born. He must have an heir, after all. 'Twas the same with me own faither. Me sister Margaret an' I have different mithers."

That stirred a memory in Ella's mind. "So…the history books got it muddled. It was recorded that Sir Colin lived with his first wife, Lady Mariott, without the benefit of marriage. It was in a book I had in my bag the first time I came here."

"Aye, I ken," Callum's voice seemed to be drifting away as Ella fell asleep. "I found yer bag. Sir Col wants ye to explain certain letters in the print to him. He's had the book in his keeping since we found it. But we never saw a charm stone."

Ella pretended to be asleep, grateful for the chemise hiding the old leather thong around her neck.

***

It was Ella's first time waking up next to a man. All of the modern-era history books had assured her that medieval couples copulated to beget children and slept chastely with their shift gowns on and the bed sheets pulled up neatly to their chins, but nothing about the life she woke up to in the morning with Callum could have been further from the truth.

He woke her with a kiss. "Losh, lass! I missed ye for so long. Can ye no' tell?"

She could tell, and as much as Ella longed for a bathroom and a toothbrush, she longed for his touch far more.

Afterward, Ella got her question in first. "One of the lads told me the household is divided."

Callum had swung his long, muscular legs over the side of the bed frame and was rubbing his eyes with his hands. It was little gestures like that which made Ella realize that no medieval wood panel or tapestry in the modern era would ever be able to portray how incredibly normal human life was in 1453. Last night, Callum had looked at her strangely when she had gotten the year wrong. Yuletide and Twelfth Night had come and gone. It was mid-March, with a green spring to look forward to.

"Och aye." He stood up, stretching and yawning before moving to the washstand in the rounded alcove of the room; they were in one of the tower turrets, and there were no corners. Rubbing water on his face and neck and then rinsing his mouth, Callum continued. "There was nay goin' back for me an' Duncan. I cursed him to damnation and promised to see him there if I had me way. His Lady mither took exception to me tone, promising to carry her tale to the priest - a pious toady of hers, a fellow by the name o' Archibald. I was within an ambsace o' calling hellfire down on her head too, but me uncle stepped in to call a truce." Callum looked down at the laces as he tightened the neck of his chemise. "Y'see, I have never thought much o' payin' court to a maiden afore…ye were me first. Duncan knew this well, a fact that urged him to carry out his base persecution o' ye."

His eyes traveled to the blood stain on the sheets, a thoughtful expression on his face. Then he laughed. "I had no' kent ye long, Ella, afore I was champin' at the bit for Faither Archibald to come trottin' over the mountains so that we might be wed."

Ella thought about translating the words 'you and me both' into the old Scots English dialect but gave up. "You had no wife because you were living at the barracks?"

Callum gave her a quizzical look. "I had nay goodwife, lass, because I am yet young. I have nae even reached me prime."

Ella grinned. "You look prime to me. Will Faither Archibald be staying at the chapel here or the manor house?"

Callum shrugged. "We must travel downriver to discuss oor marriage with me faither, Laird Stewart, afore we set up hoose. I dinnae care about the priest."

Ella giggled as she thought about how a modern era man would act if he had to wait for his parents' permission to wed and have intimate relationships. Callum smiled when he heard her laughter. "If ye will break me heart and dress yerself, Ella, we can meet with me uncle in his chambers. He wants to talk to ye more than anything else in the world."

He helped her dress, moving around behind her and kissing the back of her neck as he tightened the lacings of her kirtle. "Uncle Col wrested yer clothing from the Lady Margaret afore she could display them to the priest," he told her. "But as for this," he lifted the scrap of her old sports bra out of the pouch strapped to his belt, "I will keep it as me talisman."

He showed her how to pleat the folds of his plaid before he laid down on the ground and belted it around his waist. "Wearing a plaid in such a way is verra warm, sweetheart," he told her, "but we add hose and breeks in winter, an' during battle."

"Why?" Ella wanted to know. He placed her hand on his shoulder before he began walking down the steep turret stairs ahead of her. "So we have more hiding places for oor weapons." Callum replied in a cheerful voice.

Chapter 7

They reached Sir Colin's chambers without Ella falling all the way down the stairs, even if she had tripped and had to clutch at Callum's back in an unladylike and frantic manner. She was not sure if it had been the pointed toes of her shoes or her long kirtle that caused the small fall, but from the calm way Callum had steadied her descent, Ella supposed it was just one of the hazards of medieval life.

"Gather up the kirtle like this," Callum showed her how to clutch the long panel of material in the front of the dress at its mid-way point and then hold the fold under her bustline. "And don' stamp down wi' yer feet like that - step all dainty-like, with yer toes goin' point first and turnin' yer heels inward slightly."

Ella felt silly but knew walking gracefully was one of those middle ages things that she would have to get used to. Sir Colin was seated behind a large table and waited patiently for them to sit down. An inkwell, quill, mending knife, blotting sand, and parchment lay on the table within reach of his hands. There was a book by his elbow that Ella recognized.

It was the first time Ella had the chance to really look at the knight without fear getting in the way of her observation. He was a tall man, stooped in the shoulders, with a craggy, weathered face. He looked to be about sixty-five years of age, but maybe this was because of the wide sheaths of white running through the black parts of his hair. His expression was unreadable, so Ella trusted Callum when he told her that his uncle was on their side.

"I am at your disposal, sir," Ella said, folding her hand on her lap.

Pushing the book toward her, Sir Col pointed to it and read. "'The Breadalbane Muniments associated with the Black Book of Taymouth: Their Relation to Highland Heroes, Myths, & Legends.'"

"It was printed two hundred and fifty years into your future… and three hundred and twenty years away from my time," Ella said in a measured tone.

"Aye, that much I could read." Sir Colin almost snapped. "And I could work out from those strange garments ye were wearing during yer last visit that ye were no' from oor time or place. But I want ye to read a particular part of the book to me." With shaking fingers, the knight turned over the pages until he reached the one he wanted: Black Colin and the Lady of Loch Awe.

"Read it," Sir Colin commanded, so Ella did. It took a while, but not as long as a proper translation would usually take because many of the words were the same. After finishing, Ella closed the book and pushed it back to Sir Colin's side of the table.

"The book has it wrong," the knight sighed, raking his spindly fingers through his iron-gray hair. "I did nae break the stone in twain until me darlin' Mariott died."

Ella did not know what to say; the knight's pain at his first wife's passing was so acute. "Wh-why did you put such a powerful charm-stone in a place where someone could steal it, sir?"

In a sudden gesture, Sir Colin pushed his chair and stood up, pounding the table with one heavy fist. "Someone?! Someone, ye say?! It was one o' yer cursed ancestors who took me beloved's amulet!"

The room seemed to grow smaller as the implications of one of her ancestor's actions began to sink in. Callum took her hand, saying to his uncle in a soothing voice. "Belike, however Ella had naught to do with that, Uncle."

The knight sat down heavily, covering his face with his hands. "I don' ken, lad. I don' care. Me Mariott is gone, gone forever…"

The young couple waited for the knight's paroxysm of grief and despair to die down. If they had witnessed such an outburst one year ago, they would not have understood, but Ella and Callum had a better understanding of love and loss since spending the night together.

After a long, shuddering sigh, Sir Colin began telling his side of the story. "The tale is correct in the main - the MacGregors named the glen 'Urchy' until they were finally defeated and the folk were allowed to rename it in their own tongue as Glen Orchy. The Campbell clan has long been allied with the Stewarts at Bonawe. Laird Gerwain Stewart is Callum's faither; he had three daughters for me to choose from back then. Callum, ye are Laird Stewart's son from one of his vassals, just like yer sister, Margaret. I courted Mariott for three years before her faither allowed the banns to be read."

This did not surprise Ella. After all, Callum's sister, Margaret, was about to be betrothed at the age of twelve. Even if a marriage was not consummated immediately, a nobleman would feel more comfortable having his teenage bride living under his roof where he could keep an eye on her virginity.

"Lady Mariott died too soon before she could give me a child. It was then, in my grief, that I caused the magick charmstone to be cut in twain." The knight rubbed the sharply etched cheekbones of his face, pulling his features into a mask of sorrow. "To think that I fell for a trick that would take me away from me darlin' wife for so many long years. I swore a sacred oath in front of the blackguard oath to help the Pope launch his war. Faugh!" Sir Colin spat to the side as if to rid his mouth of some bitter taste.

"Why was the silversmith not affected by the magick when he touched it?" Callum wanted to know.

"Why would he be?" Sir Colin raised an eyebrow. "I was the master of the stone. It came to me. More than fate or luck was involved when I found it, and I suffered more than words can say in those foreign lands. That is a tale all of its own - how the Grand Master of the Knights of Saint John prevented me from returning home to Loch Awe, not even when I begged him on my knees and groveled on my belly."

Callum interjected. "Aye, an' all that drivel aboot ye forgivin' the Baron. As if a Highlander would forgive a man tryin' to steal his wife!"

That made Sir Colin smile. "Aye. I slit the knave's belly from throat to groin. It was his deception that made me swear an unbreakable oath. It was the stone that opened me eyes to the lies of the church and how the church leaders use midden muck-like oaths to control us. I swear I will never be so fooled again."

Ella was relieved she had someone like Sir Colin on her side if Father Archibald tried to get too inquisitive about her origins. The knight continued. "Not only did the stone bring me back to Glenorchy at the precise location where I was needed to resolve matters hastily, but the stone seemed to want to stay with me…"

"I know what you mean," Ella said, "My gran felt the stone's pull from the moment she inherited it from her brother, almost as if they are sentient"

Sir Colin nodded slowly. "Listen well. Mariott's tomb was sealed. An' I told no one about the stone...I-I was only goin' to set me affairs in order, and then I was going to reunite the stones. I believed that wherever my sweetest wife was if I touched the stones together, then they would have the power to unite us in heaven."

"Put your affairs in order?" Ella was confused. "But you had no heir!"

The knight shrugged. "What did I care? Laird Stewart suggested I make Callum me heir. He is Mariott's half-brither after all. But when I returned to the tomb a few days after Mariott's internment, the seals were broken and the stone was gone..."

Sir Colin's regret was palpable. "I threw the countryside into an uproar. I wanted the thief found, but then a stranger came to the watchtower and asked me for an audience. He was a sly-lookin' fellow, with keen eyes and dark aura-"

Ella knew exactly the look Sir Colin was describing. She had seen two men with the same appearance: one of them had been Mr. Satellius and the other was the man on the shores of Bonawe.

"He spoke to me in private, demanding the other charmstone from me. I spoke to him thusly: 'Sirrah - ye have me property an' ye will nae leave here alive without returnin' it.' But the man just smirked, saying: 'Sir, the boot is on the other foot. The stone in its entirety belongs to me an' my brethren. Ye have done irreparable harm by breakin' it.'

"I was maddened with wrath by now and bellowed. 'An' who might ye be to demand this of me in me own home?' And the man says: 'I am a Knight of Khronos.' Whereupon he showed me a red welted symbol engraved on his wrist.' Jumping up from me chair, I drew steel on the bold knave, but he vanished."

Sir Colin sat back in his chair, leaving Callum and Ella to bring the story to its conclusion. Ella was slow in realizing the true end of the knight's tale, but Callum was quick to understand what it meant.

"Uncle, does this mean that Ella has the stolen charmstone?"

The room went deathly still as Ella's gasp echoed off the wood panels. "But I'm a Campbell!" she protested. "There's no way I could be one of those...Khronos people! It's *me* who inherited *your* charmstone, Sir Colin!" But even as she said it, Ella knew she was wrong. The amulet around her neck was the one that had been stolen from the Lady of Loch Awe's tomb...how on earth had her family ended up with it?

The knight shook his head firmly. "*Mariott's* stone was the dominant one, the one that was destined to seek out its mate. When I was cutting it, my skill failed me, and the top part broke away unevenly. I buried me darlin' wife with the slightly bigger stone for that very reason! Admit it. The charmstone was always in yer possession, and it has a bulge at the top of the oval that fits neatly into the chipped part of this one-"

The knight withdrew a thick leather cord from around his neck, where it had been hidden by his chemise and doublet. "I kent the moment Duncan informed me about what happened the day ye disappeared. Ye have the other stone in yer possession! When he lay on ye, the stones got too close and used their magick to hurl ye back to yer own time an' place. Once I knew that I wrested the charmstone off him. Without its mate, without the charmstone's dual nature, it is naught but a trinket, but now…I have been waiting for over twenty years for this moment to see what happens when the amulet is joined to form one once more."

"That does nae explain why the silversmith could touch it," Callum said.

"I believe the stone can only be compelled with love - the type of love I feel for me darlin' Mariott. Come now, no more lies! What happened to bring ye here an' where is the other half o' *my* charmstone?"

The hairs were standing up on Ella's arms. There would be no ducking this inquiry. Closing her eyes to recollect her side of the story, she began. "My grandmother told me to travel to Scotland. Her family came from the Scottish Glenorchy and set up a small village in another part of the world, naming it Glenorchy in honor of the original. I know that much because…because we have glass books that gather knowledge for us to read. Aye, I do have one-half of the charmstone. But only when I brought my family's charmstone to Scotland, close to the one in keeping there, that it brought me here…but I don't know why it did."

"The stone wants to return to its mistress - to the Lady of Loch Awe - she who lays cold in her tomb." From the way that Sir Colin said it, Ella had no doubt that was what had happened; she had been hurtled back in time to heal the rift in the stones.

The knight stood up, leaning over the table with his hand held out. "Give the stone back to me. It was I who found it, and to me it must be returned."

"I don't have the stone here with me," Ella blurted out, desperate to think of a way to delay the inevitable. Her gran would turn in her own tomb if she knew Ella had meekly surrendered the New Zealand Campbell's family heirloom to a man who looked as if he was barely skirting on the edge of sanity. "Callum, you know where you found that book, the place from whence I came yesterday evening? That's where the other charmstone is - buried beneath the cairn."

"Uncle, the shores of Bonawe are not far from here. Ye need no' be too hasty to fetch the charm." But Sir Colin was no longer listening to his nephew. Striding around to her side of the table, he gripped Ella by her hand. "There's nay time to waste! Call for a boat, Callum! We will row with the tide."

Bowing, Callum scratched the palm of Ella's hand and lifted his chin toward Sir Colin so that Ella knew to curtsy herself out of the room. The young couple left together.

"I think ye handled that verra well, lass," Callum gave her a wink.

She was outraged. "What? That was a nightmare! Why did you let me walk into that interrogation with my eyes closed?" Ella could feel the beginnings of a temper tantrum coming on. "You did not tell me about Sir Colin's suspicions or his mad theory about one of my ancestors stealing his ruddy wife's necklace!"

Ella's cheeks were burning with rage as they walked out into the half-finished cobblestone yard and toward the loch. Callum looked shocked. "Lady Mariott's cheeks have no' been ruddy for over twenty years, Ella."

"Odd bodkins, Callum," Elle fumed, "stop being so literal!" She halted, dragging him to a stop by the hand. "Tell me what they do to witches, Callum!? I forgot to look it up online." She waved her hand in front of her face impatiently, too worried to apologize or explain the modern terminology that had crept into her speech.

He looked grim. "I'll no' sully yer pretty ears with such horror, sweetheart, an' nor need ye bother to wonder. I'll no' allow any such thing to happen to ye." Callum told her firmly. "And nor did me uncle take me into his confidence as to why he was so interested in meeting up with ye again. Look upon the bright side o' the hill - Duncan no longer has the stone now that it is back in my uncle's grasp."

Ella was not entirely reassured and fumed and stewed as she tried to remember the best words to show her displeasure.

Placing his fingers in his mouth, Callum whistled loudly and waved when the urchin came running from one of the stonemason's cottages. "Hie, lad! Who owns the boat that lies yonder?"

"It's the one I came in yesterday evening," Ella said drily. "The fisherman who brought me hither must be waiting for the tide to drift him back home."

"Then that is the one we'll row to Bonawe," Callum said cheerfully, grabbing Ella's hand and kissing it. "Come, lass, chase yer megrims awa'. As soon as me uncle has the stone, the sooner we can move on to broachin' the subject o' oor marriage to him. What complaints d'ye have to say to that?"

"Only that it's *my* magick amulet, not yer bloody uncle's!" but Callum's charm was infectious and Ella could not help but respond to it. A smile replaced her pout. "Let's visit your father while we are downriver. He might want to know about your bride before we tie the knot."

Ella had researched how couples married in the fifteenth-century Scottish Highlands. An ancient custom called hand fastening was practiced, where the couple held hands, and a length of cloth was knotted around it to show the unbreakable bond. In her opinion, it made a lot more symbolic sense than slipping a ring over the finger.

"I dinnae care what anyone thinks o' ye, sweetheart, let alone me faither. I have nae seen the auld goat from one year to the next." Callum growled, pulling her closer so he could lay a series of light kisses on her neck and collarbone, "Wild horses would no' have the strength to pull us apart."

As his mouth came dangerously close to brushing against the charmstone's cord around her neck, Ella could not help thinking that there was one thing so powerful that it would have no problem tearing her away from Callum: the magick of the charmstones. She must stay as far away from Sir Colin as she could.

A young apprentice trudged past them to fetch water from the loch with which to bind the mortar to build the wall. "Trot inside, Will," Callum asked the boy. "Go fetch Sir Colin - bid him hasten if he wants to catch the tide out."

Dropping his pail, the boy went to relay the message. Trying to push her concern about the charmstone out of her mind, Ella submitted willingly to Callum's embrace. She found it endearing that they were doing what every young couple in love was doing across every permutation of time and space: kissing passionately to pass the time in the most pleasurable way possible.

"Cut that out," Sir Colin huffed as he walked past them on his way to the boat. "Ye have nae even formally announced yer betrothal."

"Twill no' be long, Uncle Col," Callum said, taking Ella's hand as they strolled after the knight.

"Halt!" a loud voice shouted behind them. "Or wilt ye flout and flaunt yer hatred o' the church for all to see!"

Chapter 8

Ella turned to see a decrepit looking priest mounted on a donkey. At first glance, the man seemed benign enough. However, when she looked closer at the expression on the man's face, she could see the pallor and creases of cruelty and overindulgence etched into the features.

Behind him were ten men-at-arms, with some of the men wearing Duncan's emblems and the others clearly affiliated with the church because of the crosses painted on their shields. On the priest's right hand rode Duncan on the same chestnut horse he had been riding all those months ago when he returned from the King's court.

Sir Colin turned at the priest's shout, but when he saw who it was, all he did was scoff and spit onto the grass. All ten men-at-arms gasped at the knight's gall, their spears angling toward him.

Callum sauntered forward. "Well-a-day, Duncan. Have ye come to play? Did ye no' have enough last time?"

Duncan spluttered. "You can't bully me anymore, cuz, not now that I represent the church's authority." He twisted his head to indicate the ten men standing behind the horse and donkey.

Loosening the sword hanging behind his back, Callum stepped in front of Ella. "How now, so ye brought yer wee companions to play too? And are they willin' to back ye in this madness?"

Duncan looked to the priest. "Do you see how he flouts my authority, Faither Archibald? Callum, the son of a vassal wench from the Stewart clan, talks me so saucy."

Father Archibald held up both hands, sliding off the donkey and landing on the soft grass with a soft thud. "Once this is resolved, I am sure Callum will be more than happy to return to Stewart Lodge in Bonawe - his *rightful* home," he looked over at Callum with what he believed to be a winning smile. "Is that no' so, Callum? You are a Stewart and would do well to go back to being one."

All Callum did was make a sudden threatening step toward the priest, which made the elderly man squeak and run to hide behind his donkey.

"Och, awa' wi' ye," Callum scoffed. "I'll no' bite ye, Faither. I was only feinting. Come, let us be on oor way. I name meself Campbell at me uncle's request - me half-sister Mariott was happy enough to take the name, so why should I no' be?"

"Take one step toward that boat, cuz, an' the men-at-arms will be given the command to stop ye." Duncan said, "Word came to us last night that yer witch had returned. She must stand trial."

He pointed to Ella, but that only made Callum push Ella behind his back, and he continued to stand with one arm around her while the other one held his sword. Now that she could understand the language better, she could tell that the priest and Duncan spoke a much purer form of Old English than Sir Colin and Callum did. The new arrivals spoke with little to no burr or Gaelic intonation. The contrast between the accents was marked.

Sir Colin seemed to be torn. He knew that Ella had told him where the charmstone was, but he was not willing to go there on his own only to find out she had been lying. Nor did he seem to like the idea of rowing forth with a small group of righteous men-at-arms chasing after him. Sighing, he stepped in between the two groups.

"If we promise to follow ye to the manor house - I gather it's from there that ye are comin' - will ye swear an oath that we will no' be taken awa' from there until the archbishop has made a ruling?"

Only Ella and Callum were able to see when Sir Colin looked over at them, he gave a brief wink with his eye.

"You want us to hold the trial in the manor house's great hall?" Duncan and the priest exchange satisfied glances to one another. They had never dared to hope that it would be this easy. "Very well. You can fetch horses - the distance might tax the witch's stamina."

Two men-at-arms jogged to the stables to saddle three horses. It was then that Ella could see the men were wearing different tabards to the ones worn by the men at the castle. Two factions had formed since her disappearance - Sir Colin's and Lady Margaret's. It was inevitable with all this talk about the true Lady of Loch Awe that Duncan's mother would get her nose put out of joint, and this was the result.

Strangely enough, Ella was not that worried anymore. Only she knew that she still carried the charmstone around her neck just as Sir Colin did. If things became too dicey, she could just go back to her own time.

Is that the sort of woman you are, Ella? You would allow your partner to reap the fallout of your magick while you flipped back to modern times on your own? This was meant to be a one-way trip, remember?

Waving away the horse when it was brought to her, Ella climbed up in front of Callum's saddle, leaning her head against his chest and riding with her arms around his waist. Duncan saw this and shot her an evil look.

"Why so thoughtful, lass?" Callum cuddled her as he held the reins. "Ye don' believe I would allow these knaves to harm ye? This is still me uncle's fiefdom."

She laughed nervously and pushed all thoughts of running back to the twenty-first century aside. "I have no faith in the church's mercy since-" She was about to tell Callum about the Spanish Inquisition, St. Bartholomew's Day massacre, and the Salem Witch trials, but she did not. "Since the priest seems to have taken Lady Margaret's part in all this."

Callum scoffed at her fears. "Nay man would dare to withstand me uncle, sweetheart. Belike ye dinnae ken him well enough to understand his power and influence."

"It seems like that darn priest and Duncan have a fair amount of influence too..." Ella muttered, but all this made Callum do was urge his horse into a canter so that they were the first to arrive at the manor's gatehouse. He hailed the guards with a friendly grin in a way that gave Ella some hope. If Callum was so relaxed about entering the lion's den, who was she to quibble?

The sentry saluted them. Callum was still their captain after all. "What's all this to-do?" Callum asked the man. Ella pricked up her ears so she would not miss a word in translation.

"Not too many days back, the priest came barreling over the mountains on that donkey of his, Cal, bringing four men-at-arms with him. He came in response to a message from the Lady Margaret, of that I have nae doubt. Duncan came oot to greet Faither Archibald, trailing six boon companions with him - the same wastrels that followed him back here from court. They proceeded to change their tabards to show allegiance to one another, makin' much show and noise, prating about throwin' off the shackles o' yer uncle's tyranny an' other such nonsense. The messages have been flying to an' forth for a wee while noo. The Lady has hardly been downstairs, so much time she has been spendin' in her chambers, writing to this one an' t'other. We believe her to be makin' a move to gain her son's inheritance."

Callum nodded, his mouth drawn into a stern line. "What?" Ella prompted him to say something. "What? Is it bad news?"

He did not answer her. Instead of going through to the great hall, Callum waited in the courtyard for his uncle to arrive. When Sir Colin finally entered through the gates, Callum went to hand him down from the saddle, whispering in the knight's ear. "Only ten."

Ella, who was sticking to Callum's side like glue, overheard this and tried not to panic. Five men-at-arms against Callum and five against Sir Colin? If the midden muck hit the fan, she did not like those odds.

Raising her hand to his mouth, Callum kissed her hand for the last time. "Come lass. Fear not. I don' forget that I have loved ye with all me heart since the first time I saw ye."

That declaration made Sir Colin spin around frowning, but he said no more as they entered the great hall.

Lady Margaret made herself scarce. After making her curtsy to Sir Colin without eye contact, she crooked her finger, and all her ladies-in-waiting left the great hall. "Why is she not staying to accuse me?" Ella whispered.

"Wheesht, lass," Callum frowned, giving his head an unnoticeable shake. "She will nae dignify ye by acknowledging yer presence."

Without knowing it, Ella began fingering the charmstone around her neck.

Father Archibald went to sit at the head of the table on the dais with Duncan on his right side and one of Duncan's chief toadies on the left. The three men conferred in whispers as they waited for the scribe to set up his parchment and quills and for any interested bystander to make themselves comfortable on one of the benches. When the scribe clerk gave the signal that he was ready, the priest began.

"After innumerable messages were sent to my parish at Glen Orchy and further afield, the bishop commanded me to make all haste to Kilchurn Castle tower to sift out the truth of this matter. To wit: Duncan Campbell, son and heir of Sir Colin and Lady Margaret, observed a phenomenon that indicated to him and other observers, most forcibly, that the woman claiming the name of," here, the priest glanced down at the document in front of him, "Ella Campbell, did disapparate in front of their eyes."

Ella was desperate for Callum or Sir Colin to shout the accusations down, but they did not. Sir Colin stood stony-faced and rigid while Callum seemed not to even hear the words Father Archibald was saying; he stood up straight to attention with his hands resting lightly on the pouch hanging from the middle of his waist.

Ella wanted to shout out her innocence, but for the first time in her life, words failed her.

Running one finger down the parchment in an almost erotically charged manner, Father Archibald looked up at Ella. "Is it not true that your name derives from the word for 'fairy maiden'?"

This was a startling direction for her interrogation to begin with. Forgetting every police drama series she had ever watched, Ella nodded. Like every teenage girl in the modern era, she had looked up the origin of her name online. "Aye, but-"

Father Archibald held up his hand to stop her reply and turned to the scribe. "Let the document show the witch answered 'aye'."

"Why do you not have a saintly or Christian name?" Father Archibald resumed speaking, his oily tone made Ella's skin crawl.

This time, she would not fall into any more verbal traps. "I believe my origins have already been documented. I suggest you read them."

That made the priest scowl. Duncan leaned over and whispered something in Father Archibald's ear, and for a few moments, the three men seated at the high table conferred. "Very well, Duncan Campbell and his mother have witnessed the story you told them. Thus, you are a slave's girl, a runaway slave from the Norse lands."

"I didn't run away. I was abducted by pirates."

"And through all of this...activity, you managed to cling to the knowledge of your clan's name?"

The only answer Ella had for that was a nod. The priest made the usual gesture to the scribe to indicate he must write her reply.

"Now, we must move on to the accounts of those men who witnessed your disappearance."

Duncan stood up and began to speak. Ella wished with all her heart that he did not sound so convincing.

"My men and I were-"

Finally, Callum held up his hand. "Me cousin must be forsworn afore he offers his testimony."

Duncan blanched and opened his mouth to complain, but Father Archibald must have gotten the truth from Duncan during his confession because he said, "I believe we can dispense with the reasons why Duncan was waiting in the forest. Suffice it to say that he was there. You can swear your oath, Duncan, and then begin your testimonial from the time the girl touched you."

It took a while for one of the priest's men to bring in a small wooden box. "These are the finger bones of Saint Andrew. Swear on them."

"Open the box," Sir Colin demanded. "I want proof these are saintly bones." The man brought the box closer to the three people standing in the middle of the hall. Ella was given a brief glimpse of glossy browned phalanges lying on a velvet pillow before the lid was closed. With a pious expression on his face, Duncan swore his oath with his hand on the box. "I swear that when I touched the witch - or rather I should say that when she touched me - she vanished. There was nothing more of her but air."

Four other men stepped forward, took the same oath and made the same statement. The truth of their words was so obvious that not even Ella could object to their veracity.

Callum and Sir Colin's attitudes did not change, but Ella could feel the doubt and fear creeping into her expression.

"It is your turn to tell us the truth," the priest looked at Ella in a calculating way. "Swear your oath and tell the truth."

Finally, Ella would be able to have her say. Placing her hand on the box, Ella knew she would have no trouble lying while she was touching a box of bones. But from the look on Callum's face, she could see he still clung to his old beliefs. As for Sir Colin, his face wore a neutral expression with no trace of terror that her lying might invoke the wrath of some long-dead saint.

"I went deep in the forest by the loch - to set up a privy. Duncan and his attendants were waiting for me inside there. Originally they were to watch me as I departed, but Duncan chose the chance to press his attention on me in an unwelcome manner. So shocked was I that he would use a maiden in such an unseemly fashion that I bolted swiftly away. I got lost in the forest and so progressed onward back to the north, taking ship from one of the more genteel ports - where the men treat their ladies to more gallant behavior. After recouping my forti- tude, I returned. If you doubt me, there is a fisherman docked at the loch who will verify this."

She risked a look at Callum and was pleased to see the pride in his eyes. Not even a modern-age actor could have given such a mas- terful performance as she had just done. A few of Lady Margaret's ladies-in-waiting who had come to hear the trial whispered among themselves, some nodding, some shaking their heads.

Ella could tell from the way the priest's mouth closed into a thin, grim line that her story was not only plausible but like to be far more believable than Duncan's own tale. There was no more conspiratorial whispering up at the high table. Caressing the parchment with a regret- ful touch, Father Archibald stood up. "I must send word to the bishop. His word and advice are required during such serious matters." He pointed a bony finger toward Ella. "I believe ye to be a wicked woman, acting in an unbridled manner at every chance. You have been seduced by the diabhal, by his phantasms and illusions. I believe you to be a disciple of Diana, Hecate, and Beelzebub! It is those entities that have given your dull nature its cunning edge."

Callum moved closer to Ella, putting his arm around her shoul- ders. Sir Colin turned and began to stride out of the hall. "Stay!" Father Archibald's voice rang out, its echo dulled by the tapestries hanging over the stone walls. "The girl will be put to the test tomorrow. A witch does not respect the church enough, to tell the truth over saints' bones, after all."

The great hall tableau froze. Sir Colin made eye contact with Callum, giving a short shake of his head, and Callum's hand dropped even as it had risen to grip his sword's hilt. Ella opened her mouth to ask what the priest's words meant but stopped as Sir Colin shrugged his shoulders in a bored way. "However ye want it, Priest. The girl means naught to me. Put her to the test."

With every sinew and tendon in his jawline and throat jumping as if they were stretched to breaking point, Callum asked in a similarly nonchalant fashion. "Where will these tests be?"

The priest and Duncan whispered again, then: "The smell of burning flesh must not taint the manor's stores of food; she will be taken outside, to the place of her vanishing, and tested there. May the saints and angels bear witness."

"Och, verra well. Shall we meet ye there in the mornin'?" Sir Colin did not much care what happened to Ella, and this could not have been more obvious in his behavior.

"The girl must stay here, locked in the cellars."

"Then my uncle and I will stay with her too!" Callum looked like a bull about to charge with its horns down. Father Archibald waved a careless hand. "As you will. It's not likely you will be cold with those great wolf pelt cloaks you have wrapped around you."

The priest gave a signal, but it was not needed. Callum and Sir Colin were already dragging Ella to the cellars.

Chapter 9

It was inconceivable that Sir Colin would allow himself to be locked up and treated like a prisoner in his own manor house! It was impossible that Callum would stand by and allow this to happen! After all his promises and light words about Lady Margaret's cohorts not daring to cause trouble, the knight and his nephew had submitted willingly to their incarceration in the freezing underground vault.

As the cellar door yawned open onto the black crypt once more, Ella felt her knees buckle underneath her. This could not be happening to her for a second time! The first half a dozen or so cellar steps could be seen in the faint light coming through a window, but the rest of them were obscured by darkness.

"Down ye go, lass," one of the guards said to her in a respectful tone. Callum and Sir Colin were still armed after all, but what good were broadswords when their enemies were up in the great hall, probably quaffing wine and celebrating the vanquishing of their foes at this very moment!

The guard gave a slight bow to Callum and Sir Colin. "As for ye two gentlemen, it is no' necessary to accompany the lass doon there. The Lady Margaret would no' be adverse to providing beds for ye for the night."

Holding Ella up by her armpits, Callum shook his head. "Nay, Ross, I thank ye, but nay. I am so convinced of Ella's strength to maintain the truth that me uncle an' I are more than happy to share her quarters. 'Twill only be for one night."

So, down they went. Sir Colin descended first after wresting a torch from the guard and telling him to begone. "I'll no' forget this, lads," he said gruffly, looking at each man's face carefully as if to imprint their faces on his memory. "I am laird an' master here and over all the land as far as the eye can see. If ye think the soldiers an' villagers will pay their taxes an' set forth to war for anyone else but me, ye're much mistaken in the matter." Drawing himself up to his full height, the knight warned them: "I rule this loch an' land, no' that skamelar mummerkin, Archibald."

"We're only followin' orders, Sir," the men said, saluting their laird to show him that there were no hard feelings. "And from the sound o' the lass's testimony, she's likely to stand tellin' the truth in the teeth o' the testin'."

Ella wanted to scream that that sorry excuse was still being used by cowards and psychos five hundred years into the future, but she was too shocked and exhausted by what had just happened. Her feet stumbled down the last steps, and if Callum had not been holding her up, she would have fallen sprawled out next to the sacks of peas and shallots.

He lifted her into his arms, carrying her over to a sack of feathers for stuffing mattresses and placing her down gently onto the plump jute hessian as the knight placed the torch in the sconce. "Ella will nae stand the test, Uncle," was the first thing Callum said. "No one does."

"What test?" Ella's teeth were chattering, but she was not sure whether it was from cold or terror.

"They will splay ye oot over hot coals and use the same to burn certain parts o' yer body. If ye continue to tell the truth, they will cease their questions an' yer test will be over." Sir Colin told her in a level tone, giving the sputtering torch an anxious look.

"Wh-what does that even mean," Ella was bewildered. "I'm sorry, but I don't speak Torture."

Callum answered, missing her sarcasm. "They will tie ye up naked by the ankles and wrists to resemble a spread eagle. They will attach the end of the cords to stakes in the ground, positioning yer belly over a hot fire - it is there to remind ye of the eternal fires o' hell. Every time they ask ye a question, they will take a stick out of the fire and burn a certain part o' yer body. If ye don' answer, they continue to prod ye with the hot end o' the stick; if ye do answer with what they believe to be the truth, they move on to the next question. If they believe yer reply to be false, they burn ye with the stick. No one survives the test because they keep stoking the fire until ye are cooked."

"Don' forget that if the priest believes ye to be screamin' with undue indecorum, he walks away and only returns after a while has passed." Sir Colin told Ella in a matter-of-fact voice. "But once the skin has cooked to red flesh, I'm told there is no more pain."

An eerie calm overcame Ella. She prepared to tell Sir Colin about her charmstone and return back to the modern era. She doubted if she would ever go back to the middle ages because she wanted to see if Callum could come with her this time. Surely he would prefer to stay with her there in the modern era than for them both to live during such a barbaric time. Torture, slowly burning women alive, accusing people before they could defend themselves; Ella hated this middle ages craziness.

She had to choose her words carefully. "Tell me something: why is it that you - both of you gentlemen - have never asked me about what my time and space is like? Why does it not fascinate you?"

Callum was seated next to her on a jute sack and looked over at his uncle to reply, but the knight shook his head, so Callum said, "It is no' a humble thing to do…to imagine oneself belonging to another time or space."

'What's pride got to do with it?' Ella said in English, then she put the words into context for the men sitting next to her. "Humble? Why would it not be humble to imagine life in five hundred years' time?"

"Because it would put me humors oot o' balance," Callum said. She could see a slight smile on his face by the flickering light of the torch in the sconce. "If I believed the world to be full o' wonders, I would get melancholy havin' me life now, and no' then. If the world ahead o' time is hellish, it would set me heart alight to travel there to go an' set things right. Either way, I would be disgruntled with me sweet life here an' now, lass - God must have put me here for a reason."

"Aye," Sir Colin chimed in. "I would nae wish to yearn for something so beyond the boundaries that God set me - an' ye, Ella, seemed happy enough to come back here, albeit afore all this nonsense happened. That doesnae say much about yer prospects five hundred years hence."

"I thought you did not-" Ella began to say, but Sir Colin cut her short. "If ye mean to say that ye presumed me to scorn the Creator, I must say I do not. I only scorn the church. And I only abandoned me faith once during me time crusading, an' that was when I received word the Grand Master in charge of the Knights o' Saint John was fooling me. Since then, I have seen great wonders, such godly magick and miracles that I doubt not there is a Creator of it all."

"I think we're going to have to use some of that magick and miracles to get us out of here." Ella stood up, ready to drag the charmstone cord out from under her chemise.

Sir Colin stood up too, but it was not to take out his charmstone too.

"Come, Cal. Help me haul these casks awa' from the wall."

Callum went to help his uncle push the heavy barrels of ale and wine. "Bring the torch," Sir Colin ordered. Ella went to fetch it and held it aloft so that she, too, could watch the knight. Using the light the torch provided, Sir Colin began to count the stones set in the wall.

"Just one o' the reasons I caused to have the manor house so well stocked with vittles an' beer." He set his shoulder to a portion of the wall and pushed. One of the stones moved. Callum bent down next to his uncle and heaved his shoulder against the large stone. The effect of the two men's' strength was immediate. A gaping hole appeared as the stone swung inward, first as a crack and then as a large gap.

"That should be enough for the lady to leave through," Sir Colin said, standing straight and looking around the cellars with a satisfied grin on his face. "But will it be enough for ye, nephew? Such a great hulkin' brute ye've grown into."

Pushing his uncle aside with a laugh, Callum began to leverage himself through the gap. "Watch me. Even if I have to strip meself bare an' slide through naked usin' grease from the tallow catch, I will leave this blasted cellar afore that dastardly priest can get ahold o' Milady."

Sir Colin helped Ella through the hole, and Callum caught her before her feet touched the bottom of the tunnel. She had been struck dumb by what was happening. One moment they had been discussing how badly the smell of burning flesh would taint the food stores, and the next moment she was standing in some kind of a dank sluice tunnel, watching the strange sight of Sir Colin sliding through the hole with his plaid pulled around his shoulders.

"I dinnae want to see yer auld arse ever again, Uncle," Callum laughed, handing the torch to the elderly gentlemen after the knight had jumped down to stand beside them. Adjusting his plaid to cover himself and resuming his dignified attitude once more, Sir Colin replied calmly. "Och, ye're lucky I didn't come doon face first - ye woulda got yer eye poked oot."

And so, on good terms with one another once more, uncle and nephew led Ella down the tunnel.

***

Gray daylight let Ella know they had reached the end of their escape route and there was literally light at the end of the tunnel. Sir Colin told them that the tunnel mouth ended close to the castle, in the shade of the rocks on which the watchtower was built, but there was another route that took them into the copse of trees where Duncan had tried to ravish Ella. The dell where it had happened looked completely different in springtime, and the place had lost its air of menacing melancholy.

Sir Colin stood up straight and stretched and cricked his neck when they stepped out of the low tunnel, but he was in a remarkably cheerful mood for all that. "I dragged the barrels into place an' closed the gap in the wall, but we only have until tomorrow afore the dastards sound the alarm. Not to mention that with all these mysterious disappearances, the priest an' Duncan might start to connect it with the charmstone I demanded of him."

"We'll have to row against the tide," Callum said after climbing down from the tree he had scaled to get the lay of the land, wiping the palms of his hands by dragging them over his plaid. "Yer fisherman has left, Ella, but we'll have nay problem findin' another boat. I will nae leave anyone here exposed to danger though."

Sir Colin seemed to consider this advice. "Verra well. I'll send some lads across to the manor hoose this evening. Who shall they alert in the barracks?"

Callum rattled off a list of names of soldiers loyal to him and his uncle. "Tell them to take everyone captive tonight, after the last candle's wick has been pinched out."

"The priest too?" Sir Colin pinched the grizzled stubble on his chin. "I would fain no' poke the bishop in the eye."

Callum grunted. "Belike he dinnae ken what auld Archie was up to. The priest's predilection for poking maidens with hot sticks is no' widely spoken of…what say ye to postin' guards ootside his chamber with naught news to give or take? That might drive the meddler mad with curiosity."

The two men agreed to this, but Ella was not having it. "Begging you gentlemen's pardon, but are you telling me that…evil man is to be punished by being made to sit in his bedroom?!"

She pulled Callum aside. "I'm too shy to say this in front of your uncle, Callum, but we have some insights into men like Father Archibald in my time, and they are not to be tolerated!"

"What would ye have me do, sweetheart?" Callum said, "I cannae go against me uncle's advisement or the bishop."

"I know he gets off on it!" Ella sputtered in English, switching to Scottish to better make her point. "That priest was looking forward to torturing me! That witch stuff and test nonsense was just his way of getting his grubby hands on my naked flesh."

Sir Colin chimed in. "The lass speaks the truth, but how about we debate such matters after we have put some great lengths of loch water between us and this place."

"Aye, lass," Callum gave Ella's hand a squeeze, "let's be off to Bonawe. I'll set ye a compromise. When we come back, I'll let ye rule on the priest's case."

And with that, Ella had to be content.

Chapter 10

There was no doubt that there was a spy at the Kilchurn watchtower. It was eventually decided that Ella would cover her new clothes with Callum's plaid and bid one of the stonemasons to send for a long-boat to be left on the shore for them. Every stonemason and craftsman was loyal to the laird knight as it was he who paid their salaries.

Callum had no problem unbelting the plaid from his waist and handing Ella the long length of woven wool. He even helped her drape it around herself in the same manner of one of the Glen Orchy peasants: the bulk of the wool length gathered around her waist and the extra length hanging down behind her legs before it was lifted up and turned into a billowing hood and shawl when clutched in front with one hand.

They had dressed one another that morning, so there would never be any embarrassment between them again - to the point where Ella knew she would soon have to give up her maidenly shyness and find another hiding place for her charmstone as Callum was sure to beg her to remove her chemise the next time they bedded. As for Callum, his chemise was long enough to hide his dignity when they both emerged from the bushes.

"Och, could ye no' have asked the weaver to make that lawn chemise a wee bit less easy to see through, Cal," Sir Colin said after observing the casual way Ella and Callum accepted one another's new apparel.

"D'ye want to take me place then, Uncle?" Callum chuckled. "This spring air has a wee nip in it, so help me."

It was at moments like that when Ella realized the uncle and nephew had a very close bond. Their free and easy manner around one another reminded her of family teasing. She felt sad for Callum that he had that bond with his half-sister's widower husband and not his own father. She guessed that Laird Stewart must be quite old and, after doing a few calculations in her head, worked out that Sir Colin could not be more than fifty-three years old. How the poor man must have suffered while on a crusade for him to have aged so precipitously.

"Hunch the wool over yer shoulders, sweetheart, as if ye've had a hard day toiling in the fields and pull down yer kirtle to hide those new shoes o' yers.."

Imagining what it would have felt like to rise at dawn and spend the rest of the day bending down to plant seeds, Ella adjusted her posture.

"Aye, that's more like it. Noo, hobble down to the wall and ask for Will's faither. Tell him ye are sent from Sir Col an' we need to escape without observation. Ask the man to scurry doon to the kitchens an' bring up some ale an' bread to put in the boat. But he's to wait until nightfall before doin' the boat."

It happened just as Callum predicted. Wee Will ran to fetch his father, and the stonemason recognized her under the heavy hood. "Och, we kent that priest was up to nay good," the man scolded. Ye're in a good place to return to, Milady. If anyone sees ye, they'll think ye search for kindling. Please tell oor laird that the boat an' vittles will be there come nightfall."

No one suspected the hooded woman wearing the old clan plaid. While she waited, Ella ate part of the stonemason's small beer and bread rations. They were generous enough rations and she did not feel guilty drinking and eating the small portion she was offered. When she noticed the bird-like quality to the bones and tendons of her wrists, Ella realized she had lost weight, a considerable amount of weight from the look of things. Tapping her cheekbones with drumming fingertips, Ella gauged she must have lost around ten to fifteen pounds or around six-odd kilograms. She was tall enough to handle luscious curves, but that kind of weight loss was worrying.

Casting her mind back over the last three or four months, Ella could trace the steps leading to her current scrawniness. The cause was grief, followed closely by shock and neglect; her double life was getting in the way of her health, and now that she was stuck in the middle ages, there was zero chance of her regaining those lovely plump curves of her youth.

She reached her hand out and took another of the stonemason's bannocks, promising to take better care of herself in the future.

It was an unsettling feeling thinking that one of Lady Margaret's spies might be staring down at her from one of the watchtower windows. Standing up, she asked Will to lead her to his mother's cottage. These makeshift structures would be cast down after the stonework was finished, and the masons and their families would return to their real homes.

The woman's accent was so strong Ella found herself simply nodding and smiling as she sat on a short stool by the fire, but it was a relief to be out of observation from the tower. She took a bowl of soup from the woman after being told it was made from vegetables. As much as Ella had tried to force herself into the idea of eating snout to tail, she could not yet convince herself to do it.

In London, she had gone to eat at one of those restaurants dedicated to cooking and eating every part of the animal but had not been able to eat half the things put in front of her. She could just about handle the fact that sausages stuffed with finely minced heart, lungs, kidneys, and liver were edible if enough strong herbs and spices were added to the mix, but when a plate of tripe and onions appeared on the table, floppy, wobbling and gray, she had thrown in the towel. When a customer next to her table had begun to tuck into steamed goat head, she had run to the cash till with her throat clenching.

When the man at the till had asked her if the meal had been to her satisfaction, Ella had replied politely. "I'm sure I'd eat most of the food if I was blindfolded, but some of the smells are horrendous. The smell is *warning* me not to eat it."

But that had been in the days when she never knew how it felt to have hunger pangs grip her stomach. Closing her eyes, Ella imagined eating offal if she were starving, but her rejection of it was the same.

At nightfall, she joined Callum and his uncle at the boat. Once they were launched and a good way from the shore, only then did Sir Colin allow her to speak. "Callum, do the poor folk eat every part of the animal, do you know? It is what my time believes to be true - that the peasants eat every part of the animal: eyes, brains, anus ."

After shooting her one of his humorous smiles, Callum replied. "We have hounds to feed too, Milady. Why would the peasants eat foul-tasting parts of the animal when they can give it to the dog? Then the dog would be strong. And if it is a hound, it will set forth the next day to catch a tasty rabbit for its master's pot."

"So…peasants don't eat the rear end of a pig's arse and cow udders?"

"Are ye mad, lass!" Sir Colin raised his voice, now interested in the conversation despite himself. "Why would we kill a perfectly good coo? It's like me nephew says - the hounds must eat well, and it's them that gets the umbles. If we dinnae feed oor hounds, they would ravage the forests an' byres. A good huntin' dog can bring down a covey o' ground birds or a whole warren o' coneys!"

Chastened but wanting to share her experience, Ella told the men about her time. "In my time, it is generally believed that peasants were given the inedible parts of a carcass that no one wants so that they have meat to eat too, and no part of the animal goes to waste."

To this, Callum and Sir Colin only chuckled, shaking their heads in disbelief. "If I treated the poor folk like dogs, lass, they would depose me. An' none o' oor animals go to waste either because the hounds get the tainted parts - believe me. Oor villagers have more than enough meat to eat, believe me; most certainly in summer when the excess o' male lambs and calves are marked for slaughter."

Ella was not done yet. "Hang on! Many tribes - they are like clans - serve goats head at banquets, and the brains and eyes are delicacies, I promise you!"

More guffaws of laughter from the men. Taking pity on her, Callum told her the reason: "Belike the men began to eat that food as a test o' their manhood, sweetheart, and it grew from there to become a tradition or feat of strength. I'll allow ye that there is some good eating on the head o' a goat: the cheeks and neck; nay man would put something foul-tasting in his mouth unless he were a braggart or a fool."

And with that, Ella had the answer to the twenty-first-century fascination with people eating the most disgusting parts of an animal.

Their lighthearted conversation took them downriver to Bonawe. Sir Colin warned Ella upfront as the boat hull scraped the beach shingle in the shallows. "Heed me words. Laird Gawain had three daughters from his wife an' no others. All the other young folk that claim kinship with him-" here, he jerked his head toward Callum, "-are his busterts, born from vassals an' local women. Dinnae broach the subject to the laird head-on. If he wants to tell ye the origin o' Callum's mither, he must do it in his own time."

Ella couldn't imagine wanting to broach that subject to anyone. She helped the men push the boat all the way up the beach. "We must cover it with brush and no' leave it within sight o' the river, uncle." Callum grunted; he was pushing the bulk of the boat's weight forward.

"Och, they'll have better things on their minds than to think aboot followin' us, Cal." Sir Colin shook his head, but there was a satisfied look on his face. "Oor soldiers are stormin' the manor house at dawn."

Ella smiled at the thought of that creepy old priest waking up with a thicket of sword points bristling around him.

She waited for the men to drink and sup on the vittles the stone-mason had left in the boat. When she saw them ripping the bread with eager hands and gulping the ale out of the leather firkins, Ella was re-minded how little first-world twenty-first-century people knew about true hunger pangs and how stoical medieval folks were about hiding it if they were starving.

Modern era people bounced seamlessly from one meal to the next without much anticipation or enjoyment, instead of using food as fuel to get them through the day.

When it came to her body, Ella knew she would have to re-edu-cate her stomach to eat when the opportunity presented itself because she would never again be assured of regular meal times or any other instance of modern comfort.

One by one, they ambled into the woods that grew close to the beach to relieve themselves.

"Noo, let's get on with visitin' this faither o' yers, Cal," Sir Colin growled, checking the leather laces tied around his boots were tight.

Callum did not answer. His hand was held up in a gesture of si-lence. Ella froze; even this early on in her Middle Ages life, she knew better than to whisper, 'what's going on?' after Captain Callum Camp-bell gave the order for silence.

Many heartbeats passed before Callum eased his sword out of the scabbard slung behind his back, and he raised his voice to command. "I kent ye're tryin' to hide in there, fellow, so quit yer skulkin' an' come oot."

Ella remembered the brigands and the crossbow. She badly wanted to run to Callum and push him out of the way. Instead, a man emerged from the thicket of trees with his hands held up in the air, a sly, supercilious grin on his face. "Hail and well met auld friend," the man said to Sir Colin. He turned to wave at Ella, saying in English,

"We must stop meeting like this, Ella Campbell. People will start saying we are in love."

The man ignored Callum, even though the braw young warrior was holding a sword in his hand.

Sir Colin sighed. "Och, a'right. Let's get this over with."

***

"What gave my presence away?" The man asked Callum as they moved further into the forest. The young warrior ignored the question, keeping Ella on the side, furthest away from the man.

A bundle of kindling was already set up in a fire pit. The man had been waiting for them. Without asking permission, Sir Colin sparked his tinder flint onto the moss embedded in between the dry twigs, pointing to the wood and saying, "Ye give away the fact ye have lodgings close by."

Saying nothing, only giving one of his quirky smiles, the stranger sat down on a log, rubbing his hands toward the flames and waiting for the others to sit down.

"I gather you have returned to search for the other stone?"

The man spoke Scots so they could all understand. Sir Colin shifted on the log. "There are but two halves o' the whole. Forgive me if I dinnae tell ye where ye might find t'other."

Ella tried not to look guilty, but her consternation at the man's words could not be held back. "I-I don't understand…where is it?! I forgot-!" It had completely slipped her mind that she had taken both the charmstone from the museum and her own stone with her in her mad dash to reach the Glenorchy charmstone display cabinet.

She jumped up, pushing Callum's hand away from her as he tried to pull her back down.

"What?!" Callum had to show his annoyance at Ella smacking away his hand. "What are ye rantin' on aboot, lass?"

Walking to the man by the fire, Ella grabbed his dark doublet sleeve so he could not disappear again. "Mr. Satellius…he told me to bring the other stone with me - *and I did*! B-but it was not with me when I landed! I never thought much about it! But I know now - I remember! I took both pieces of the stone with me! I swear I brought them here. And yet, in the water, there was only my own stone." Ella's confusion did not abate, but her voice grew softer as her furious thinking overwhelmed her.

All the man did was laugh. "Aye, like I said before, my friend Mr. Satellius did his job well. Finally, the loop is closed."

"Speak sense, sirrah," Callum growled, "or ye might be speaking it with me sword at yer throat."

The man stood up and gave Ella's shoulder a comforting pat. "Come, Ella Campbell. You did the right thing. Allow me to introduce myself: I am Zatlath and my counterpart is Satellius."

Sir Colin grumbled. "I'm no great scholar, but I ken yer friend's name means 'attendant' in French."

Callum shook his head. "In Latin, the translation is closer to accomplice or even 'he who assists,' Uncle."

Ella stayed quiet about what the word meant in the modern era; she was still too shocked that she had completely forgotten the moment when the two stones had joined and she had grabbed hold of both of them, but only remembered bringing one of them with her.

"So, what does the name Zatlath signify?" Sir Colin enquired.

"The word Satellius is from Latin." Here, the man nodded toward Callum. "My name is of Etruscan origin: it means 'he who fetches the axe.' "

"I'll no' be lyin' when I tell ye that I don't much like the sound o' yer name, lad." Sir Colin remarked, but the light tone he was using was not fooling anyone.

"Be at peace, Sir Knight," the man said, "all my name means is that I am the servant who runs to fetch the weapon for his master when the enemy presents itself." Zatlath held up his hands toward them in a placatory gesture. "Here's the truth. Listen well. This girl, Ella, has been lying to you. She holds the stolen charmstone in her possession. Can you not feel it? My friend, Satellius, told her to bring both stones with her from her time in space, but it is the nature of the stones that she could not remember the stones melding, which is why she forgot the event. When she attempted to bring both stones to this time and place, it closed the loop. Now, the stone no longer exists in her sphere, she will no longer be able to return there. Sir Colin, it is you who holds your own stone, and it is this woman who holds the one taken from your lady wife's tomb."

Finally, Ella found her voice. "Let me get this right: so long as I could touch my stone to the one here or touch it to the one in the Edinburgh Museum, a loop in time existed."

The man teeter-tottered his hand to show Ella her guess was not quite accurate, replying in English. "Think about it like this. If you had been able to bring *both* stones back here, how would you explain Sir Knight still holding his stone at this moment in time? There cannot be three halves. When you tried to bring both stones back to a time when it would mean three halves of one whole existed, it was that impossibility that closed the loop."

"Three halves of one whole cannot exist," Ella translated the words for Callum and Sir Colin.

Zatlath smiled and nodded, pleased that she had been so quick to grasp his explanation. Speaking Scottish again, he said, "Aye. But now that your ability to go back to your time is over, tell me, Ella, do you feel lucky? Perhaps a more accurate word would be - do you feel blessed? Remember, you're going to have to stay hidden for longer this time."

"Hide? From whom?" Callum asked.

Chapter 11

"Hold yer tongue, lad! If I am to follow what ye are saying correctly, this woman has my property." Sir Colin stood up and moved over to where Ella was crouched on her log. "Hand it over. Yer family were thieves, I knew it!"

Callum shook his head. "Uncle, I'm beggin' ye to keep a calm head on yer shoulders. Let this man finish speakin'." As an aside to Ella, he grinned, saying, "I'll have that chemise off ye next time, lass, or did ye hide the charmstone in yer pouch?"

Sighing, Ella surrendered her secret. "It's on a cord 'round my neck. Please let's listen to what Mr. Zatlath has to say before we start arguing over the stones."

"You should listen," Zatlath said. "Aye, I'm talking to you, Sir Knight. That day in the Land of the Saracens, you found something that was not meant for your touch or sight or understanding."

Sir Colin sat back down. He was as interested in hearing about the stone's origins as Ella was.

Standing by the fire, Zatlath began to speak.

"Satellius and I are not Knights of Khronos. We are servants to the stones. To fully understand, we must go far, far back in time and space. First, why do we call it time and space? You, Ella, most especially, will want to understand this. To do so, we must return to the ages before the great ice, for that was when we learned about the nature and essence of time.

The earth and all the planets and stars are not fixed in the universe. The entire body of stars and planets circle ever upwards in a great spiral. In the vastness of space and time, there is no returning to the same point - the mass of space and time spirals up and up as one great vortex.

Do you doubt me? Then you do not understand the vast nature of space. It is in a state of constant flux, like a cosmic dust devil, like a hurricane, twisting up and around like a tornado. The vortex started very small but got larger and larger as the timeline expanded."

"I have seen such things in the desert," Sir Colin said, "these twisting cones of sand and wind."

"Aye, so believe me that the universe is the same, and where you exist is just one grain of sand within it. No planet or sun is ever again in the same place or at the same time because of the never-ending spiral upward into the heavens.

Around twelve thousand years ago, a group of those who commanded the world with magic discovered the strange nature of time and space. They discussed it because it irritated them that the world was so.

'Why should we not create something that can drop back down through the spiral?' they asked one another, 'Why should we not command time and space to bend to our will?'

"These were perfectly legitimate questions, given the great knowledge these magicians possessed. For a long time, they had defined the three-fold character of the gods of time thus:

There is Khronos: the god who represents the unavoidable nature of time - the past, the present, and the future. He is the embodiment of the empirical facts of the timeline and all its linear associations, traveling from birth to death.

There is Aion: the god who represents eternal time - the unfathomable concepts of eternity and the afterlife, the cyclical nature of the seasons, the years of dryness and the years of flooding, the centuries that bring heat, and the centuries that bring cool. Khronos and Aion are allies; they are part of the human experience, no matter how little they might know or understand about the Great Spiral of Time and Space.

And then there is Kairos. Kairos is unique and stands alone. Kairos is a friend of wizards and witches. Kairos represents time in relation to *opportunity*.

Think about how important time is to fate. Winning or losing; meeting the one person with whom you will fall in love; meeting an accident or avoiding it. All these things are under the rule of Kairos. But Kairos favors two types of action in particular, namely: the actions that must be taken in order to achieve something great, and the direction one must take in order to find their one true love."

Trying hard not to sound like a modern-era atheist stereotype, Ella interrupted. "Hang on - there are no gods. I'm sure even Sir Colin and Callum will agree with me on this."

The man shook his head. "I do not use the word 'god' in its literal sense. But there are beings: spirits, great unseen forces, and entities, that hold great influence within the confines of this universe. Knowledge of them was lost after the coming of the ice.

Now, when the magicians discussed the essence of Kairos, they grew concerned with what persuasive arguments Kairos might have used as a tool to motivate any desired outcome. How many of the actions leading up to an opportune result involved the hardship of others? For example: what if the joining of two true lovers caused a third-person heartache? What if, on the way to achieving something great, one person caused great suffering to others?

Other magicians disagreed. They said that the simplest way to look at the triple nature of the time gods was to think of them in an agricultural sense, and it was for that purpose the gods were always designed: Khronos ruled the years, Aion ruled the seasons, and Kairos ruled the opportune moments to sow and reap.

But that was not the end of the discussion, as you know. Before the ice came, our civilization and its magic were mighty. It was not long before a way to overrule the laws of the spiral was found. It was a complicated ritual, and it involved a mystical rite where he who wields the stone must dedicate his life to it. The stone must mean more than life or death to the magician who chooses to use it. After all, traveling back through time is the greatest adventure one can have, but no one should do it on their own. In effect, the magician married the stone."

"You're joking!" Ella burst out in English, but Callum bid her to be quiet. "Wheesht, lass! I have nae heard a story told so well since oor bard died!"

Zatlath continued.

"The stone was melded, bonded to the magician because they had to swear to love and cherish it forever. Only then did the stone have the motivation to drop down through the vortex at the command of its master...nay, that is the wrong word...a better word to use would be 'partner.'"

The man used the Scottish word for 'spouse.' Then he continued, choosing his words carefully to narrate his story better.

"Each stone would drop through the spiral vortex so long as someone who cherished it was traveling alongside it. After a while, the stones seemed to form an allegiance to a particular tribe or to the family of he who wielded it. You cannot doubt me now, Ella?"

Ella could not stop shaking her head and scoffing. "I wasn't in love with *anyone* when I went to Edinburgh and entered the museum." Turning to Callum, Ella asked him to corroborate her. "Tell him, Callum. Tell him that I was - that I had never had a lover before you."

Zatlath shook his head. "Yes, you are...you always were. You were in love with Callum Campbell. That's how the spiral and the stones work. We don't know why, but the stones only answer to the command of love; they see it as a great chance to do great things. It is possible that the stone saw a chance to return to the place where Lady Mariott was born or that it saw you as the best way to return to its family. We have an imperfect understanding of how Kairos works, but think about it - he is the god of *opportunity* - the chance for someone to take control of their fortune and become the master of their own destiny."

Sir Colin uttered a groan. "Please don' tell me that when I found that stone - *my stone* - that I was stealing someone's sweetheart or some other unnatural explanation."

Zatlath looked somber. "Alas, that is where much of our discourse disagrees - half of the Knights of Khronos believe it was your great love for Lady Mariott that helped you find the stone. It is exactly the kind of thing Kairos would want to happen. But the other half of the Knights support the magician who wants his stone back. Satellius and myself have been sent to warn you and guard you against the magicians who call themselves the Knights of Khronos."

"Hang on," Ella raised her hand the same way she might do in a classroom. "Isn't the stone broken? Sir Colin cut it in twain."

The man shook his head. "It seems that once the stone was severed, the love charm between Colin and Mariott was severed too, and that just made the stone begin looking around for its next couple."

Ella felt faint. "So...what you are trying to tell me is...that over five hundred years later, the stone felt that Callum and I would make a lovely couple, and that is why all of this midden muck is happening to me?"

The servant of the stone nodded, happy she finally understood. "Aye. True love is rare."

"But-but how did my family end up with the other half of the stone?" Ella was confused.

"Because ye're descended from one of the guardians for the Knights of Khronos. They have been waiting all these years for the stones to be activated by love, and now that they have been, they will come."

"Who took the stone from Mariott's grave?" Sir Colin scowled.

"The Bishop of Rutherglen; Father Archibald is one of the priests under his command, I believe. The Bishop was induced into helping the Knights of Khronos, not one day after you returned home from the Crusades. In exchange for gold, the Bishop has sworn to act as the stone's guardian. They were waiting for the stone to be abandoned since you found it, Sir Knight."

"I never abandoned me wife's half o' the stone!" Sir Colin was outraged. The man shrugged. "Walking away and leaving a stone is considered to be abandoning it - a great betrayal; likewise, losing the stone is seen as Kairos' way of taking it away from you.

"It was the Bishop who removed the stone from Mariott's tomb. His cousin, Glynnis Campbell, is part of the Campbell clan, is he not? It was deemed safer for your wife's half of the stone to remain in Campbell hands until the stones were joined by love once more. Remember what I said about stones remaining faithful to their families? And so that is how it got passed down to Ella's family."

Sir Colin made a scoffing noise but then quietened down again when Zatlath continued speaking.

"As I said, the stones only work when love is involved. Once they have linked to those who love, the stones will do anything to protect them. That's the beauty of love: Kairos knows this. Our biggest opportunities happen when we are in love - children, family, home."

Callum smacked his hands on his thighs before standing up. Only then did the other two listeners around the campfire realize that they had been sitting enthralled for hours. Stretching and yawning, the young warrior said, "Och, Zatlath lad, I'm of a mind to believe ye. How is it that ye can hang aboot whenever an' wherever ye feel like, by the way?"

"I love the stones and have sworn an oath to protect them. Thus, I am allowed to move freely through the Great Spiral between all of them. The magician who lost the stone that you found, Sir Knight, accepts Kairos' ruling, but many doubt his word."

Sir Colin scoffed and spat. "Dinnae talk to me aboot oaths. How am I to get that cursed Bishop o' Rutherglen off me back? He has the King's ear and much influence, ye understand."

"Can't we just give the stones back to the Knights of Khronos now?" Ella suggested. "I mean, how bad could it be? I'm related to their appointed guardian, after all."

"Are you mad or foolish?" Zatlath frowned. "These are powerful magicians beyond your comprehension. They despise Kairos and all he stands for because they believe he taints the purity of linear time! When they find you, they will see you as part of the problem...!"

"Enough of this chat!" Pounding his hand on a tree trunk so hard all the brown winter leaves fell down around the campfire, Callum's voice echoed through the wood. "This is all useless speculation until I have more proof! Come, we must march to Laird Stewart's gatehouse this night."

"You mean your father," Ella prompted, hoping for Callum to speak about his real father with more affection, but he ignored her.

"Dinnae fash him right noo, girl," Sir Colin whispered to her as he helped Zatlath kick the fire out. "Cal must feel a wee bit wretched after hearin' aboot that five hundred years wait o' yers."

Callum and Ella went back to the cairn next to the abandoned brigand camp and dug out her backpack. "Hoots, lass, this thing weighs more than a one-year-old ox!" Callum remarked, but all Ella said by way of reply was: "Hurry, I'm worried that your uncle will do something horrible to Zatlath in our absence! I don't think he enjoyed that story as much as you did."

Having spent the previous night sleeping fitfully in her new surroundings in Callum's arms, Ella did not hold up well on the march to Stewart Lodge. She fell several times - a few times from exhaustion and a few from accidentally falling asleep on her feet - but most times, she fell after tripping over some root or pothole in the dark, having her foot press down onto a gaping hole and that awful lurching rush of fright until her foot found solid ground once more.

The incidents happened often enough for Ella to have a fair amount of adrenaline coursing around in her system to keep her awake until they reached Stewart Lodge.

"We're here," Sir Colin told Ella, poking her in the ribs. "Look lively."

"Where else would we bloody well be," Ella grumbled, rubbing her ribs, but she was beyond happy to reach the safe haven they had been marching for. Since hearing Mr. Zatlath's revelations, she had been expecting to hear the Bishop of Rutherglen chasing them down with hounds, both Bishop and hounds well-fed from all the offal they had been eating. Or maybe she was so tired she had been dreaming on her feet?

Callum took her hand. "Ella, I don' need some Sassenach comin' here an' tellin' me that we're meant to be together." Pinching her chin to tilt up her face, he kissed her, muttering the words so that she could feel them on her mouth. "I love ye."

Giggling, her tiredness and bewilderment forgotten, Ella whispered. "Oh, Callum. I love you more than anything or anyone. But I don't think Mr. Zatlath is a Sassenach…"

Ella said over her shoulder, "Are you Etruscan, Mr. Zatlath, or Greek?"

But the man was gone.

Chapter 12

It was not exactly a warm welcome they received at Stewart Lodge, but they were given sleeping quarters by the laird's steward when the sentries woke the old man up and introduced him to the lodge's new visitors.

"I vow it is almost time for Matins, Sir Knight," Steward Martyn told them as he bustled around with an obviously irate housekeeper, making beds and pulling out bolsters.

"I thank ye for yer kindness, Steward Martyn and Madam Chatelaine." Sir Colin dipped two fingers into his pouch and brought out two coins, giving one to each of them. "Worry no' overmuch to fetch us from our beds at dawn. It will please me nephew and his woman to sleep later. But do inform me dear brither, Laird Gerwain, of oor arrival upon his waking."

Ella was shocked to find that Sir Colin was to sleep on a truckle bed that had been pulled out from underneath the big bed, and Callum and she were expected to sleep on the bed itself in the same room. "Aren't we being rude?" she whispered into Callum's ear, remembering how often Gran Campbell had told her to be polite and considerate to her elders.

Callum grinned. "Nay, lass, but me uncle is being verra gallant. It is usual for all three o' us to sleep up on the bed, but he makes way for us to join oor bodies at will if we are so inclined."

Swallowing down her opinion on middle ages ideas about privacy, Ella stripped down to her chemise and allowed Callum to help her climb into the bed. She noticed Sir Colin's eyes following her, but she knew that it was only so he could look at the charmstone cord poking out at the top of her neck.

"Are you sad to know the stones answer to Callum and me now, Sir Knight?" Ella asked sleepily as her head lay on the soft feather pillows.

"Nay," Sir Colin muttered. "I am only sad that me darlin' Mariott is gone."

Callum snuggled close to her, nuzzling the side of her neck with his mouth. Ella was just about to launch into a harsh criticism of medieval morals relating to the bedroom before Callum said softly. "Fall asleep as fast as ye can, lass, else me uncle's snores will wake yer dead ancestors."

The couple did what all young people liked to do in a new environment. They laughed softly together about the absurd revelations of the day before drifting into sleep.

Sir Colin never snored at all, nor did he sleep. He was mourning the final loss of hope to be reunited with his great love, Lady Mariott.

***

They slept late, but when Callum and Ella awoke, Sir Colin's truckle bed was empty.

"Let's hope he's gone to smooth the way ahead o' us." Callum muttered as he flexed the wrists and shoulders of both arms to loosen the muscles, spreading out his fingers before bunching them into fists. "I don' wish to waste me day re-tellin' auld Zatlath's story."

Ella wished she had spent more time hiking over Highland hills and mountains instead of trying to learn how to weave and embroider online. Her muscles ached and throbbed. A wave of nostalgia for the twenty-first century swept over her as she realized the way was shut, and her internet access and nonsteroidal anti-inflammatory drugs were gone forever.

"I don't think your uncle would risk doing such a risky thing. The Bishop of Rutherglen might have spies everywhere."

Pushing Callum away from her when he tried to kiss her good morning, Ella explained her modern-era dilemma. "I want to clean my teeth and wash my face first," she insisted. That made Callum scratch the bristles of his beard in a thoughtful way. "Is there aught that I should do the same? I have been too lazy to learn the customs of yer time, sweetheart."

Ella stood on tiptoes and gave him a kiss on the cheek. "Nay, love, it is what women like to do in my time."

"I am sure ye look bonnie enough withoot worriting aboot ablutions, Ella," Callum told her, and then he headed out the door.

Ella was about to shout for him to stop. She didn't like her chances of finding the lodge's great hall without his guidance, but she remembered an image of a castle online and the layout of the floors. After doing her ablutions to the best of her ability - which included using one of her hairs as dental floss - Ella walked downstairs.

Stewart Lodge was a vast, sprawling structure with fully three wings and many cellars. Fortunately for Ella, all of the cellars were built under floorboards and needed two strong men to lift the portals to access the freezing stone caverns underneath, and there were only two floors with no way to reach the rooftop. She eventually found her way to the great hall. The small mirror she had withdrawn from her pouch in the bedroom told Ella that she was the epitome of medieval female decorum.

Her hair was rigorously scraped back and hidden under a tight, white linen scarf. Her face, particularly her forehead, shone out under the hood she placed over her head, like a large big oval moon. Her eyes looked preternaturally large without the benefit of dark eyebrows and eyeliner. Her neck seemed to rise like a swan from the edging of the kirtle and tunic that swept from her shoulders to her bustline. Remembering what Callum had taught her, Ella carefully picked up the front of her dress in the middle and brought it under her bosom. The hemline trailed behind her as she walked up and down the stairs, making pleasant rustling noises.

Callum and Sir Colin were chatting to Laird Gerwain as she entered, and the two men hailed her to come closer. "Come, lass," Callum said, "ye are welcome at me faither's high table without the benefit of marriage. The strict moral codes of the kirk hold nay sway here."

Ella hesitated. She was a modern-era woman: why did what Callum had just said rankle her? Millions of people lived and died in the twenty-first century without bothering to get married, but it bugged her Callum seemed to take it for granted that she was on board to remain his girlfriend.

Sweeping an elegant curtsy, Ella approached the dais at a stately pace. "Forgive me, Callum, but I deserve a place at any high table due to my merit alone - I don't need to bruit my association with you to earn it."

The three men at the table were struck dumb, and the rest of the ladies and gentlemen leaning against the walls of the great hall or sitting on the benches pushed under the trestle tables gasped to hear such unmaidenly remarks!

Laird Gerwain, however, liked her tone. Poking Callum in the ribs, he laughed. "The blood runs hot in this one, Cal. Ye better have a mind to yer manners!"

Callum replied with a rueful smile. "Then ye should too, Faither."

This sally tickled the laird's fancy. "Och, I wish I could say the apple does nae fall far from the tree. Come, gentleman. Let us remove to another chamber. Lady," he beckoned to Ella, "ye must come with me."

From the suddenly serious look on Laird Gerwain Stewart's face, Ella had a suspicion that she was about to hear the story of another piece in the puzzle. When she looked from the portly old man to Callum, she could see no other likeness between them other than the color of Callum's hair. Callum was built like a chieftain, tall and stern, with broad shoulders and mighty legs. His red locks tumbled from his brow in a riot of fiery color, his fingers always seemed to be searching for the hilt of his sword. Laird Stewart, on the other hand, was slightly grizzled with features that leaned more toward looking merry and relaxed. He was also a good few inches shorter.

She followed the three men through to a basement chamber. From the sound of it, the room was not too far away from the kitchens. Ella could hear the recognizable sounds of cooking pots banging down next to the fire pit and scullions bashing copper pans by the wash pump.

"We need no' worry aboot bein' overheard here, lad," Laird Gerwain told Callum.

"Why worry about being overheard at all?" Sir Colin shrugged, pulling the table into the middle of the room so that all four of them might sit around on stools. "The day when the church overrules the will of a laird is pure fiction."

"That rascally Bishop and his pestilent priest, ye mean?" Laird Gerwain said. "Nay, but what I have to say is for yer ears alone, dear friend."

Ella was fussing with placing her kirtle so that she wouldn't trip over it when she stood up, but her ears pricked up at this. Having spoken so freely to the laird in the great hall, Ella now felt a little shy. She did not want Callum's father to think she was a loudmouth.

Leaning forward in a conspiratorial fashion, the laird began to speak. "If the Bishop seeks for news o' ye, he will have it. Vassals will have stuck their heads oot the doors upon yer arrival. They might no' favor the kirk over their own clan, but that will nae stop their lips from flappin'."

From this announcement, Ella realized that Sir Colin had already told the laird about their predicament.

"However, it was nae for that reason that I dragged ye doon here." Laird Gerwain pushed his chair back from the table as if he wanted to distance himself from what he was about to say.

"Colin, hearin' aboot Duncan's uncouth behavior and his willingness to side with his mither amidst all yer trials has given me the strength to tell ye this:

Twenty-two years ago, and after ye left on yer travels south to join the Crusades, me daughter Mariott came to me. Ye had been married for nigh on five years at that time. She told me ye had waited to have bairns because of her youth, but after she reached the age of seven and ten years, ye both deemed her old enough to birth a bairn without injury or risk. But yer union was no' blessed with a wee bairn, even after many nights o' conjugal adventure.

And then ye went off to the Crusades, Col, and naught was heard from ye again. Or at least for so long that it hardly mattered anymore. It must no' have mattered to ye that ye had nae heir too, 'cause ye hastened off to war for the Pope regardless."

The laird held up his hand to show he was done when Sir Colin moved to reply. Laird Gerwain continued. "Mariott was being pestered by that dastardly Baron MacCorquondale the moment ye headed off over the hills. She told me the man had made all types of excuses not to return to his manor house on more than one occasion, hoping that Mariott would offer him her bed. Rest assured, she offered him lodgings with no access to her, but the damage was done…when Mariott found herself with child. It must have happened the night afore ye departed, but happen it did."

Ella could have heard a pin drop, the room was so silent. Pleased that he seemed to have everyone's attention, Gerwain spoke.

"The problem, o' course, was that nay one would believe Mariott's innocence - five years nae bairn and then the moment her dhuin leaves, she's miraculously pregnant. So, she hid the pregnancy for as many months as she could and then came here to birth the child."

Knowing medieval fashions for females as she did, Ella could see how easy it would be to hide a protruding belly under a high-waisted girdle and voluminous folds of the woolen kirtle.

Laird Gerwain shifted in his chair a bit. "It was well known that I had bairns with women other than me wife, so this child became one o' them. When ye came back from crusading, Col, I sent the boy to ye for fostering as soon as I could, but by then, Mariott had died during that feverish plague that swept the countryside. So did Mariott's mither, me own wife. I scratched me head to think of a way I might broach the subject to ye, but lacked the evidence. Then ye went and installed Margaret Robertson in yer bedchamber and after she birthed Duncan, ye went an' married her. I never kent when was the best time to tell ye that yer firstborn son was there by yer side all the time." The laird sat back in his chair and sighed. "Well-a-day, that's me story told. Do with it whatever ye like."

"What about a midwife?" Ella asked. "There must be some witness to Lady Mariott's confinement."

The laird shook his head. "'Twas me wife who helped her. We could nae risk a midwife carrying the tale back home with her an' causin' folks tongues to wag."

Silence. Laird Gerwain banged his fist on the table. "Hoots! Is this no' good news? That Duncan is no' yer only child? Now ye can kick his traitorous arse to high heaven and embrace the bairn ye had with me daughter, Mariott."

Sir Colin looked across the table at Callum. Father and son. Ella held her breath, waiting for the grand moment of denial or acceptance, the gleeful celebrations that might follow once father and son were reunited. It was exactly the kind of lucky scenario the spirit of Kairos would enjoy: the son of the man holding one half of the charmstone falling in love with the woman holding the other half of the charmstone - or had that been the goal all along?

Ella and Laird Gerwain seemed to be waiting with bated breath.

It was Sir Colin who spoke first. "I've always loved Callum like he was my own son. Foster son or blood son, I believe we have never needed another bond to show one another affection."

Callum spoke next. "Me loyalty an' respect for Sir Colin does nae change after hearin' this news."

Ella was extremely let down. She felt the hairs on her arms that had pulled up into goosebumps fall back down again when she realized that she must be the only one in the room to feel emotion.

"Och," Sir Colin leaned over the table to give his son a pat on the arm, "I kent ye had to get yer astonishingly good looks from somewhere, lad. So help me, but ye would have never got them from this fat auld goat, Gerwain, here."

Callum gripped Sir Colin's hand in a brief grip before replying in a similarly jocular fashion. "Och aye, I hear ye. But God save me from ending up a withered auld scapegrace like ye, Faither, or at least no' until I'm too auld to bother aboot it!"

All three men laughed hard together, ignoring Ella for the moment, which gave her time to wipe her eyes. Typical men. Just when she believed their callous behavior caused them to act indifferent to the news, all they needed was some time to process before expressing their emotions in their own way.

Seeing Sir Colin's proud bearing, tall, sparse frame, and black hair shot through with white, Ella wondered why they had not noticed or mentioned the similarities before. But this was one instance where a DNA test would not be needed.

Chapter 13

They were alone, back in the bedchamber. Since Laird Stewart had become aware of her ladylike presence, he must have ordered the servants to prettify the walls and floors for her. When Ella had walked back in, the floors were covered with two rush mats, on the walls hung tapestries and portraits, and a trunk had been placed next to the wall. Opening its lid, Ella found her backpack inside it. The blue colors, textiles, and paracord toggles looked completely alien.

"So…" Ella racked her brain to think of the right words. "Um… are you happy about being Sir Colin's son?"

Callum had flung himself into the armchair next to the empty fire grate, stretching his legs out in front of him. He had a thoughtful expression on his face. "I was always his son. It's only that I changed from bein' a foster son to bein' one born of his blood."

Ella muttered something about bloody men always being so literal before saying in a louder voice. "But you're his heir now, not Duncan. Now we can go to court and meet the king and do all the things a male heir does." Ella could not help but be pleased with the thought of visiting the court and living at Stirling Castle or Holyrood Palace. She might even get to walk the halls and corridors of Edinburgh Castle! A lifetime of banquets and velvet silken finery danced in front of Ella's eyes. The history of James the Second of Scotland was well known to her. It was the medieval equivalent of rock star status.

"I'm Captain o' me Faither's army until he says otherwise. An' even if he did ask me to journey to court and present meself, I dinnae think I would. The new clothes I would need alone must cost a fortune, and I have yet to enquire how much gold me mither set aside for her child in her dowry."

This sounded very much as if Callum was thinking about making the trip to visit the king alone. Ever since she had been introduced to Laird Stewart as Callum's woman-friend or lady-companion, which-ever word they used in the middle ages to mean a female who chose to sleep with a man without the benefit of marriage, Ella temper had been simmering. At this, her temper completely boiled over the top.

"Meself, meself, meself!" Ella shouted in a mocking voice. "Do you hear yourself!? Do you have any idea how much those words hurt me!? I'm not some floozy that you can choose to push aside whenever you want to make a decision, Callum! I'm your partner! Partner! And it doesn't bloody well matter if we're married or not! You need to consult me first."

She thought about the wondrous night they had spent together the night she returned. It ripped her soul apart to think that when they had joined their bodies together, Callum's mind had not translated that into meaning something bigger. Ripping the hood and scarf off her head, Ella screamed. "If I want to go to court to meet the bloody king, you should at least consider my request! Do you think I want to spend the rest of my life dressed like a washerwoman while I wait for you to get your arse into gear."

Even with some of her words being completely impossible for Callum to understand, he had no trouble understanding Ella's tone of voice. In a flash, he was off the chair and bearing down on her. Grip-ping her wrist, his voice seethed. "I kent it would nae be long afore ye threw the stones' decision in me face! Ye think ye might make free with the King's grace and curse his royal heid just because that dark traveler told ye we are destined to be together? Ye're an artful wench, Ella. Be done with these megrims now!"

He dropped her wrist abruptly and moved to sit back down in his chair, so Ella hit his back with her fist. It was not a sore blow, but it was an impudence beyond any medieval comprehension. Callum slowly turned to look at her, amazement making his eyes wide. "Did ye dare to raise a hand to me, woman?"

Ella was crying, sorry, tears of rage. "Why do you ignore me, Callum? Why do you resent how the stones have mapped out our fu-ture together? Don't you love me anymore?"

He was having none of that. Nor was he immune to the heartfelt nature of her tears. Sweeping her into his arms while their tempers were still hot, Callum took his lady to bed, where he was better equipped to prove his love to her in his own way. After they had vented their spleen and emptied their loins of desire, Callum swept Ella into his arms. "Honestly, lass, can ye see me tricked out in lengthy poulaines, with the toes so long they must be tied to me calves with silver chains? An' what aboot those curt doublets? Wilt ye have me show me courtly wares to all the ladies? Knowing this, why would ye see me - I mean to say, us, dressed in such unmanly garb?"

She giggled and snuggled closer to his chest. Tracing the taut bulk of his chest muscles, she was enjoying the way they felt under her fingertips. "You have a point, Callum. But when are we going to marry? It rankles me to have no standing in the community. It was bad enough that I was introduced to your - oh goodness, Laird Stewart is your grandfather now - grandfather with no title to lend me dignity."

He kissed the top of her head. "Och sweetheart, why did ye no' tell me yer dignity was hurt? From the way ye fell into me arms the moment ye came back to Kilchurn Castle, I thought ye were content to remain as me concubine."

Ella restrained herself from falling into another tantrum. She waited for Callum to reach his point, which he did soon enough. "Here's the problem: with Father Archibald imprisoned with Duncan in the cellar and the Bishop affiliated with those Knights of Khronos, would ye no' agree that it might be a wee bit difficult for us to find a kirk in which to read the banns?"

Casting her mind back to her hours of research about medieval practices, Ella remembered about banns. It was when a couple's betrothal was announced three times in church before the wedding took place, so that word of the ceremony would have time to spread throughout the community and for anyone who disapproved of the union to lodge a complaint. It was the best time for a jilted lover or spurned wooer to crawl out of the woodwork and make themselves known. It was the reason why Mr. Rochester had married Jane Eyre in secret; if banns had been read, it would have given all the busybodies time to stick a spoke in the tragic couple's wheel. In the modern era, reading the banns aloud was replaced by publishing an advertisement in the local newspapers and eventually reduced to the minister asking if anyone objecting to the couple's union to speak now or forever hold their peace.

"Do we have to order the banns to be read?" Ella said in a caressing voice. "Can we not get married in secret?"

"We would have to travel far to do it," Callum warned her. "If journeying over the mountains is somethin' ye wish to do, we may as well ride all the way to Edinburgh or Stirling to get the King's approval in person, but there's a big problem if we want to be doin' that - we'll be in verra hot water if they ask for yer heraldic achievements."

Instantly, Ella was distracted by this new medieval tradition. "My heraldic what?"

They were like any other young couple, lying abed after putting their differences aside by making love. Callum was in no mood to let Ella out of his arms just yet, so he summoned the words to describe it to her. "Well…ye have a heraldic achievement, I'm sure, but there's nay way we can lay oor hands on it. Does yer family in that other Glenorchy have a coat o' arms or an escutcheon or some other clan item?"

Ella thought back to those dusty brass shields on her uncle's and gran's mantelpieces. "Yes, I remember it was a unicorn on one side and a warthog and some crest with a feather…"

"Aye," Callum nodded. "That's similar to ours. Perhaps that hog ye mention is a boar's heid? That is our crest animal. Oor motto is 'Noli Me Oblivisci'."

"What does that mean?" Ella wanted to know.

Callum sucked his teeth for a few moments as he thought of the best way to translate for Ella. Eventually, he said, "Forget me not."

They spent a few more precious moments in bed until Sir Colin ordered a servant to pound on the door and bid them come down for dinner. There was nothing else for Ella to do except bend down to pick up her headscarf and hood again. After dressing fully, she lifted the charmstone cord off her neck and gave it to Callum.

"Why don't you hang onto this a bit? You might as well, Callum. Mr. Zatlath says its power has gone."

He was busy strapping his sword onto his back and only grunted. "It's yers. Belongs to yer family. Don' be intimidated by me unc- by me faither's words."

Standing on tiptoes, Ella helped him settle the sword between his shoulder blades and then pulled the cord around his neck. It only just fit because the cord was able to stretch. "Why must you carry yer sword everywhere with you?" Ella wanted to know. "Doesn't it get in the way?"

He shrugged, bending down to tighten the straps of leather around his boots. "As a Highlander, I can only answer ye thus, Ella: I feel naked without me sword an' me plaid."

Stepping aside, Callum allowed Ella to walk out of the bedchamber in front of them. She said to him over her shoulder as they walked down to the great hall. "But I've seen lots of people walking around without such garb and weaponry. Are they not Highlanders?"

Callum grinned as he stepped in front of her this time to push the great hall doors open for her to walk through, saying, "Let me amend that glib statement, lass - a Highland warrior feels naked without his plaid an' his sword."

They both looked up to see that Sir Colin and Laird Gerwain Stewart were not seated at the head table alone. In fact, the dais looked very crowded with people. Ella took one look at them and knew at once that she was staring at men who were not part of her timeline. The color of their clothes, and the shape of the garments, were a million times more authentic than any Hollywood costume designer could ever imagine. The expressions on the men's faces were neither malicious nor benign. It was almost as if they were supremely indifferent to the astonishment they were causing.

"Your impudence has caused us much discussion, Ella Campbell." One of the men said. It was after he spoke that Ella realized the other occupants in the hall were frozen, all except Callum and her.

"The stone belongs to me." Ella was positive that this was all just some big misunderstanding that could all be sorted out with a diplomatic resolution being the desired outcome for all.

A soft sound came from behind her. Ella was jumpy and spun around to see Callum had withdrawn his sword.

"Callum, if you love me, don't..."

It was too late. The young Highland warrior attacked. He was so swift that Ella was able to see the magicians standing on the dais open their mouths wide with shock. And then one of them moved just as swiftly to where she stood, and the next thing Ella knew, she was no longer in Scotland during the middle ages.

***

Dear Reader,

Please enjoy book 3 of The Lady Of Loch Awe Series. *Destined To Be With The Highlander.*

https://www.amazon.com/dp/B0BRLT2FY9

Made in United States
Troutdale, OR
06/09/2023

10527296R10060